Picture Perfect

Also by P. G. Kain

THE SOCIAL EXPERIMENTS OF
DORIE DILTS
#1: *Dumped by Popular Demand*
#2: *The School for Cool*

COMMERCIAL BREAKS
#1: *Famous for Thirty Seconds*

COMMERCIAL BREAKS

Picture Perfect

BY P. G. KAIN

ALADDIN M!X

NEW YORK   LONDON   TORONTO   SYDNEY   NEW DELHI

m!x

ALADDIN M!X
Simon & Schuster Children's Publishing Division
1230 Avenue of the Americas, New York, NY 10020
First Aladdin M!X edition July 2012
Copyright © 2012 by P. G. Kain
All rights reserved, including the right of reproduction in whole
or in part in any form.
ALADDIN is a trademark of Simon & Schuster, Inc., and related logo
is a registered trademark of Simon & Schuster, Inc.
ALADDIN M!X and related logo are registered trademarks
of Simon & Schuster, Inc.
For information about special discounts for bulk purchases, please contact
Simon & Schuster Special Sales at 1-866-506-1949
or business@simonandschuster.com.
The Simon & Schuster Speakers Bureau can bring authors to your live event.
For more information or to book an event contact the Simon & Schuster Speakers
Bureau at 1-866-248-3049 or visit our website at www.simonspeakers.com.
Designed by Karina Granda
The text of this book was set in Bembo.
Manufactured in the United States of America 0612 OFF
2 4 6 8 10 9 7 5 3 1
Library of Congress Control Number 2011940156
ISBN 978-1-4169-9787-0 (pbk)
ISBN 978-1-4169-9790-0 (eBook)

To the picture-perfect WBC, my love

ACKNOWLEDGMENTS

Thank you. Yes, YOU! Thank you for reading this book. By "reading this book" I mean the *entire* book. I mean, this page isn't really even part of the story of the book and you're still reading it. That really impresses me, and I'm very grateful to have such a scrupulous reader.

Not to mention that this is book two in the series, so chances are you've already read book one. You have a lot of choices in your bookstore, and I'm so grateful you chose this book. Without readers there wouldn't be books. Well, there might still be books, but we'd have to use them as doorstops or paperweights, so it wouldn't really be the same thing.

Please stop by my website, www.TweenInk.com or e-mail me at pg@tweenink.com and tell me what you thought about *Picture Perfect*. I'd really love to hear from you, and I answer every e-mail I get. Hopefully you aren't using this book as a doorstop. But if you are, I sincerely hope it's doing a good job.

CHAPTER 1

I pick up the dishrag on top of the stool, look at it quickly, and smile broadly, making sure my face is not turned too far away and that my eyes are not squinting. I look at the pert blond woman standing next to me and say, "Mom, you did it. You got those grass stains out of my cheerleading skirt."

Ashley, the pert blonde, picks up the water bottle on the stool next to her, smiles as broadly as I am smiling, looks straight ahead, and says, "I didn't do it. Nature's Way did it. And it didn't hurt the environment."

That's my cue, so I say, "Now that deserves a cheer."

I am about to actually start my cheer when from behind the camera Neil says, "Dang. This dumb camera has been giving me problems all day. Can you hold while I try to fix it?" And as if someone has pricked the surface of a balloon with a needle, our version of an ideal world immediately collapses. Our commercial audition has paused, and reality creeps back in.

I am not a big fan of reality. Why would I be?

In commercials I'm the captain of the cheerleading squad who lives in a immaculate suburban home and has a clean skirt without grass stains, a perfect routine, and a gorgeous mother who laughs and smiles on cue.

In reality my mom is a math professor who thinks prime numbers are fascinating, and when I auditioned for the middle school cheerleading squad last year I tripped over my own shoelaces, knocking down the school mascot so Marty Pinkerman's furry squirrel head rolled off his human head and across the gymnasium, ending up at Principal Conner's feet. Needless to say, I did not make the squad and have little chance of even being allowed to attend future cheerleading tryouts.

But here in the cramped casting studio, or in a commercial on TV for thirty seconds, my life is picture perfect.

Neil takes the camera off the tripod and starts fiddling with it. "Sorry, this will just take a second," he says. Ashley and I both nod, and then she bends over into some kind of yoga pose that she say helps her focus. Ashley is my absolute favorite fake mom in the world. She has straight blond hair that just brushes her shoulders, a small, perfectly symmetrical nose, and bright blue eyes that dance when the camera is rolling. I met her during a shoot for a commercial for an office supply store about a year ago. I played the daughter who couldn't decide if she wanted a sparkly pink notebook or a glittery purple one. She played the mom who let me buy both.

My dad saw the commercial last week while he was waiting for a flight at an airport in San Diego, and he actually called me right from the terminal. Even though it was about two o'clock in the morning, I was thrilled to get his call, since I hadn't heard from him in a while.

Ashley changes her pose and stretches her arms toward the ceiling. As she arches her back, I notice that her necklace slides around and dangles behind her. I know she'll want to be camera-ready when we start rolling again, so I tell her about the runaway chain.

"Oh, thanks, Cassie," she says, coming out of

her pose. She moves the chain back to her chest, and I notice the necklace is actually a beautiful gold heart-shaped locket.

"That's so pretty," I say.

"Oh, this?" she says, fingering the jewelry. "Well, I got it at the place on Eighth Street next to the bookstore. I had to. Jennifer was wearing almost the *exact* same necklace when she booked that cat food commercial, and Miranda was wearing one in that car commercial, so now *everyone* is wearing them." She opens the locket and looks at the picture inside. "I guess something about this locket screams 'young mom.' I dunno."

Sometimes I forget how supercompetitive the "young mom" category really is.

"Well, it's pretty," I say.

"Okay," Neil says. "I think we're rolling again. Let's take it from the top."

In an instant we are back at it. I pick up the dishrag pretending to be my cheerleading skirt, and we run through the lines, this time without stopping. I do a short cheer and Neil yells, "Cut!" Ashley picks up her bag, and I grab my backpack, and we head out of the tiny casting studio.

The crowded hallway is full of fake moms

and daughters reading through the lines we just finished. We are each just slight variations of the other. As always, there are a few new faces among the crowd of the usual girls.

"It was great seeing my favorite fake daughter," Ashley says, and gives me a tight hug. I delight in the fact that she thinks of me as her favorite fake daughter, but whenever she says it out loud and hugs me, I get this terrible feeling in the bottom of my stomach. The truth is, sometimes I wish Ashley was my real mother and that I was her real daughter. I feel like a terrible, evil person when I think these thoughts, since my real mother is a perfectly normal, mostly average mom who, for some misguided reason, believes that what you have on the inside is more important than what you look like on the outside—which explains why her wardrobe makes her look like an extra for *Woodstock*, the movie. I give myself a mental slap across the face to try and shake these thoughts from my mind.

"It was great see you, too. I really hope we book this one together," I tell her.

"That would be fun," she says, pulling off the headband she was wearing during the audition, sticking it in her bag, and letting her bangs fall over her face. "I'm off to my Pilates class. See you around." She glides through the crowd and makes her way out of the studios.

I decide to fix my hair in the bathroom before my next audition. The casting office I am going to for my next audition shares a bathroom with a couples counseling office, and more than once I've had to deal with mildly hysterical women while I was brushing my hair.

I walk down the hall toward the bathroom around the corner. As soon as I turn the corner, I spot the one person I am trying to avoid.

CHAPTER 2

Faith Willis is heading toward the bathroom from the other direction. I immediately stop and hope she hasn't caught a glimpse of me. Faith and I are always competing against each other for the same spots, since we have a similar "look," although I once overheard a casting director say that Faith is more "upmarket" while I am more "theatrical." I'm not really sure what that means, but it didn't exactly make my self-esteem leap in the air. I'm pretty sure Faith booked the spot for that new energy drink I had a callback for a few weeks ago, so I am desperate to avoid her.

Half the girls I audition with are supersweet and make you feel like you are part of a very cool club, but then there is the other half, who turn every callback into a battle of epic proportions. Faith is one of the high commanders in their army. I turn away from the bathrooms and walk down the hall to the elevators, thus avoiding any contact with her.

I make my way through the crowd, and when I'm on the other side of it, I hear someone calling my name. I turn around and see my friend Phoebe and her brother, Liam. Phoebe and I booked a cereal spot last year where we played two friends gossiping on the school bus. Within a few minutes of meeting each other, we became real friends. Phoebe is one of those girls who is just super friendly and supportive. I think that's why she has been booking everything lately. You can't turn on the TV without seeing her smooth blond hair and sunny smile. I couldn't be happier for her. She comes over and gives me a big hug. Phoebe is a serious hugger.

"Hey, Phoebe. Hi, Liam. I just saw your Apple-Time commercial last night, Pheebs. That dress you were wearing is so pretty. I loved the lacy skirt it had."

"Thanks," she says. "I loved, loved, *loved* the way that dress looked, but even thinking about it hurts."

"What do you mean?" I ask.

"Well you only saw the front of it on camera. They bought the wrong size, so the back was cut open just before we started rolling and they held the thing together with pins and duct-taped it to my body. That's why you never see my back and only see my face in the mirror of the vanity. It looked beautiful but felt awful."

"That sounds terrible," I tell her, but I know last-minute fittings can be brutal. Then I remember that I have to get to my next audition "I've got to run. I'm late for an appointment at Mel Bethany's."

Phoebe and Liam look at each other.

"The Maryland Lottery spot?" Liam asks as I pound my fist on the down button for the elevator.

"I just came from there," Phoebe says. She looks quickly from side to side and then whispers, "RR was in the waiting area, FYI."

RR stands for Rory Roberts, the boy currently holding the number two spot on my Crush List. And since the number one spot has been held by Johnny Depp since I was, like, six, RR is really in the highest-ranking position any mortal human can have. The elevator doors open, and I thank Phoebe for the information before hitting the *L* button for the lobby and saying a small prayer for an express ride to the ground floor. I look at my watch and realize that I still have plenty of time to make my appointment. The question is, will Rory still be waiting for his appointment and will I get a chance to go to the restroom and fix my face before "accidentally" running into him? Just once I would like to book a spot with him so we could hang out on set together. We've been at a few of the same auditions recently, but that has barely given me a chance to have any substantial interaction with him. I do, however, see him in the Mega Motors commercial pretty often.

When the elevator stops, I quickly walk through the ground-floor lobby and push my way through the revolving door. It's a sunny May afternoon, but there is still a chill in the air. As I start walking toward Broadway, I feel my cell phone vibrate in my pocket. I keep walking and pull the phone out to look at the screen. It's my agent, Honey Arbuckle. I can't believe Mel has already called my agent to find out where I am when I am not even late, at least not yet.

"Hey, Honey," I say without slowing down. "I'm on my way to Mel's right now. Neil had a camera malfunction and the elevator took forever and—" Honey cuts me off before I can finish my list of excuses.

"Listen, kiddo," she says in a raspy voice that sounds like she started smoking when she was a toddler. "Don't waste your time. You've been pulled from the list."

Sometimes at the last minute a casting company will change the call because the client changes their mind. One minute they want redheads with freckles and the next they want Latina twins over six feet tall. It's part of the business, but since Phoebe just came from the call, that can't have been what happened. "I don't understand," I tell Honey. "They didn't change the breakdown?"

"No, kiddo, they didn't," Honey tells me.

"So why shouldn't I go to the audition?" I ask in confusion.

"All I can say is that I had to pull you from the list. I gotta take this other call. Your mom will explain the rest. I hope I'll talk to you soon. Bye, kiddo." Honey hangs up, and I am just standing on the corner of Broadway and Eighteenth Street with my cell phone up to my ear and no one on the other end. For a second I consider just showing up at Mel Bethany's and pretending I never got the message, but I know a stunt like that will get me banned from the casting office for life. In my mind,

I go over the conversation I had with Honey. I don't understand why I was mysteriously pulled from the list. Suddenly I remember a very important phrase Honey said that went something like, "Your mom will explain."

That can only mean one thing.

CHAPTER 3

As I walk down Broadway past the Union Square Greenmarket, I decide to visit my mother at work to try and do some damage control instead of going directly home. If my dad was in town, I would certainly try to work on him before even thinking about going to see my mom. But a few months ago they sat me down to explain that my dad would be taking on a new sales position at his company and that would mean he would basically be living on the road most of the time, so they could have a "trial separation." I freaked out when they told me. I mean, what kid wants to see their family split up? But they calmed me down by saying that they had not made any decisions about anything and that they were going to do what they could to work it out.

I miss my dad a lot, and the whole idea of the trial separation is unbearable to even think about for more than three seconds, so I don't. At least I don't have to worry about coming home and finding my parents in the middle of a screaming match, or worse, one of their "Let's not fight in front of our daughter" things where the silence is unbearable. And even though I don't get to see my dad, at least he gets to see me, even if it is only in a commercial on TV.

When I get to Kimmel Hall, I take the stairs up to the third floor, where my mother's office is located. I can hear her talking with some student about something to do with square roots and integers. I truly can't believe this is how she spends her days. I stand just to the side of the open door, out of sight but within earshot, to see if I can figure out what kind of mood my mom is in. Before I can really assess the situation, the student she is meeting with gets up and walks out of her office. For a second I consider going home and vacuuming the apartment or washing the dishes so I have something banked in my favor, but before I can even turn from the doorway, I hear, "Cassie Marie, I'm not sure how long you plan to spend hiding outside the doorway, but I can assure you it won't change the situation." Some mothers have eyes in the back of their heads. My mother can see through walls, bookcases, and most lies.

"Hi, Mom," I say in a quiet but friendly "what situation could you possibly be talking about" kind of way as I come out from behind the door. My mom says, "Let's have a conversation in my office."

I don't know why she always calls these "conversations." Conversations are what you have at parties or while you wait for class to begin. Conversations are not lectures about taking responsibility for your actions or learning to mature gracefully.

I take the seat across the desk from her. Her office is like a mini version of our apartment. She calls it organized chaos. I just call it a mess. There are books piled on top of books, piled on top of more books. The walls of the office are covered with my mom's adventures in crafting. There is the paint-by-numbers landscape of a snow-covered mountain, the magenta macramé wall hanging that resembles a deranged owl, and my personal least favorite—a portrait of me made out of, wait for it, macaroni. The only good thing about seeing these objects here is that they are no longer in our apartment. My mom says that after dealing with numbers all day, crafting relaxes her. I keep telling her she should go to a spa or get a massage, but she refuses to listen to me.

My mother squeezes between the wall and the bookcase next to her desk to sit down at her chair. Usually I can ignore my mom's size until something like this chair reminds me that she is on the chubby side. She always says her weight doesn't bother her and that she is perfectly happy with her body. Her long brown-and-gray hair is in a braid, which she only undoes when she sleeps. If I had to cast my mother in a commercial, it would be for some weird organic vegan granola that was made without harming trees, birds, plants, or any other living thing. Of course, no such commercial exists, so the chances of seeing my mother on TV are slim to none.

My mom just looks at me for a minute before opening her mouth to speak. "Cassie, I am very disappointed in you. Your school called me to tell me that you didn't hand in your science report on the periodic table for your Foundations of Science class."

The very phrase "periodic table" makes me tense. It should be called the idiotic table. For crying out loud, it's not even a table! When am

I ever going to need this information in real life? Answer: never. Actually, never ever. I consider sharing this information with my mother in hopes that it will change her mind about the importance of this report. Instead I just stare blankly at her, since I know that there is almost nothing I can say to stop her when she is gearing up for a lecture.

"Then they tell me you told your teacher you couldn't do the report because you had an audition for a juice drink commercial." My mother says the word "audition" like it hurts her teeth to get the word out of her mouth. She has never understood that I'd rather go on auditions than spend my time after school at some silly soccer game or just IMing my friends. Never mind the fact that the juice drink commercial she is referring to was a national network spot that would have aired in over fifty markets. There is no way my dad would have not seen it.

"Cassie, this is one hundred percent unacceptable. I won't have you putting your commercial auditions before your academic endeavors. Your science teacher told me that even if you ace the rest of your exams, you shouldn't expect a grade higher than—"

"Mom, I know," I say quickly, cutting her off. The last thing in the world I need is to hear my lousy grade out loud.

"Cassie, your schoolwork comes first, which is why I called your agent to let her know that you are grounded from any auditions until further notice. So you shouldn't be expecting any calls from Honey."

"What?" I jump out of my chair and shout. "That's not fair!" How can she do this to me? She knows how important this is to me. She knows how hard I work to book stuff. She also knows that when I book, I make a substantial amount of money for my college fund. I try to use that to my advantage. "What about saving for college? What about being able to afford a good school?"

"Cassie, if your grades don't improve, we don't have to worry about paying for a good school, because chances are you won't be getting into any."

Ouch. I drop back down in my chair. Why doesn't my mother believe in me more? If my dad were here instead of traveling around the country selling pharmaceutical products, he'd let me keep auditioning. In fact, he'd encourage it. He always calls me when he sees me on TV, or at least he tries to.

My mother knows that last bit stung. She comes

around from her desk and sits in the chair next to me, putting her hands on mine.

"Look, baby, I know how much you like your go-sees and auditions and your friends there, but I want to make sure you have opportunities and options when you're older."

"But Mom, summer vacation is only a few weeks away. What am I supposed to do? Sit home and sweat?"

"Cassie, you aren't on house arrest. There are other things to do in New York City during the summer than go out on auditions. You could see Shakespeare in the Park, go to the Museum of Modern Art . . ."

"Yeah, Mom, I know. . . ." At this point I am no longer listening to her. Somewhere deep inside me, I'm sure I'm angry about her unreasonable decision, but right now the only emotion that surfaces is sadness. My mom goes on and on about how many stimulating cultural and educational experiences there are to be had in the city, and I just blankly stare back at her. I wait until I hear a pause in her lecture and try to think of something to say that will change her mind.

"But Mom, what if I only went on a few go-sees a—"

"Cassie! Have you been listening to a word I said? I just listed any number of activities to keep any kid your age busy for three summers, and the only thing you have on your mind is going out on go-sees."

"I was listening," I say, even though we both know I'm not exactly telling the truth.

"Cassie, there are no more go-sees, auditions, callbacks, or bookings. You are too preoccupied with it all, so none of it until we can figure out how to improve your grades."

I leave her office in a state of shock. I feel like someone has just punched me in the stomach or canceled a snow day. When I feel this terrible, there is only one thing to do. I walk directly to Solazzo's Bakery.

CHAPTER 4

"Oh, no. Chocolate-covered cannoli. What happened?"
Ginger says after opening the door and spotting the square box from Solazzo's Bakery tied up with red-and-white-striped string. She knows I reserve these treats for only the absolute worst problems. "Let me get my jacket." Ginger grabs her purple-and-lime-green hoodie from behind the door and we head out of the building. Just being in the elevator with her and the cannoli already makes me feel better.

Ginger has been my best friend since we met in first grade, when both of her parents came to work at NYU. I've known them almost my entire life, and both her parents are amazing. Her dad is an anthropology professor and has bright orange hair, a bushy orange beard, a booming laugh, and he knows everything there is to know about ancient Egypt. Her mom teaches creative writing, is a published poet, makes the best chicken soup in the world, and gets around using a purple wheelchair that she decorates for every major holiday. For Purim last year she strung all these brightly colored masks on the armrests and a drawing of Queen Vashti on each wheel. Ginger could not have been adopted by more awesome parents.

We live in the same faculty housing complex, but I live on the seventeenth floor of the Gould Building, and Ginger lives on the fifth floor of the Walsh Building. The courtyard of the building complex holds a small playground and park. All the kids from the building play in the courtyard, and Ginger and I basically lived in that playground when we were little. A year or so ago we decided we needed to spread our wings a bit, so now we also hang out sometimes in Washington Square Park, which is only a block away from where we live.

"Are you gonna make me wait until we get to The Bench to find out what happened?" Ginger asks as we walk across Third Street toward Washington Square. The Bench is a green wooden two-seater that is perfectly positioned between the dog run, the fountain, and the arch. We pretend we put a charm on it so that it will be free whenever one of us really needs it. Today I really need it.

"We're almost there, Ginger."

As we turn into the park, I see The Bench is free, even though the park is packed full of people enjoying one of the first warm days of the year. Luckily, a group of kids are break-dancing next to the fountain, so most people are gathered around their performance. We sit on the bench and take out the chocolate-covered treats.

Ginger puts a huge bite in her mouth and barely swallows before bombarding me with questions. "So what happened? Did something happen at your auditions? Did you book something? Was Rory at your audition? Did he catch you picking your nose?"

"Ginger!" I say, slapping her arm lightly and giggling. "That's disgusting." Ginger can always make me laugh, even though I don't think she's always trying to be funny.

"Well, whatever happened, I'm sure it will all be forgotten by your next audition," Ginger says. The crowd that has gathered around the break-dancers cheers as one of the dancers starts popping.

"That's just it, Ginger. That's the problem. There aren't going to be any more auditions."

"WHAT?" she shouts. Ginger totally gets me and knows how important my go-sees are to me.

Having a best friend like Ginger is the one thing that makes reality bearable.

"My mother has basically grounded me for the rest of my life. She's being totally unreasonable."

"I hate to ask, but does this have anything to do with the periodic table?" Ginger asks shyly. She tried to get me to tell my mother about the whole mess in my Foundations of Science class, but I didn't listen to her. And she's the last person in the world to say, "I told you so," but I know she must be thinking it.

"The school called my mother, and now she knows I'm not exactly at the top of the class in Foundations of Science. She said no more auditions until I can figure out how to improve my grades. What am I supposed to do all summer? I don't know where she thinks we're going to get the money for college," I tell Ginger.

"You could always get a summer job," Ginger suggests.

"Maybe," I say. Of course, a summer job wouldn't even come close to earning me the amount of money I could get from booking even one small local spot. Not to mention the fact that babysitting presents very few romantic opportunities and even fewer chances for my dad to see me flash across the television screen of some hotel lobby.

Still, I tease Ginger about the idea of working together. "What if we both got jobs doing something totally crazy?" I say. "Like handing out flyers for Macho Taco dressed as a burrito or something."

Ginger laughs. "That would actually be fun. But you know I'll spend the summer stuck in Chinese school." Ginger was adopted from China, and her parents make her go to Chinese school each summer so she'll always be able to speak the language from the country she was born in. Even though she complains about it, I know she secretly looks forward to it.

"Ginger, you know you can't wait for Chinese school to begin this year so your crush on Ming-wei can start up again." I have a Crush List, but Ginger is much more single-minded.

"You say that like I ever stopped crushing on him. Anyway, who wants to be stuck in summer school? It's not like the grades from Chinese school even go on my transcript."

"Yeah, you're right," I say, and lick a bit of chocolate off my finger.

Then Ginger shouts, "That's it!" and slaps me on the arm. I almost swallow my finger.

"What's it?" I ask her. "Oh, no, was there something gross in your treat, like that time we found a moth in your salad?"

"No, nothing like that, and remember you promised to never bring that up again." Ginger shudders briefly. I look at her carefully. I can always tell when she is coming up with some elaborate plan. Her right eye twitches just a little bit, and at this moment her right eye looks like someone threw sand into it. Then she says, "Cassie, I think I've just come up with a solution to your problem."

"Ginger, unless you've invented a time machine that will let me go back to the third marking period and hand in my report, I don't think there's anything you can do," I tell her.

"Oh, a time machine! That's a fantastic idea, but not the one I'm thinking of right now."

"What are you thinking right now?" I ask, not sure I want the answer.

"Well, you might not like the sound of it at first, but you'll have to admit it might just work. . . ."

I look at Ginger and her twitching right eye and prepare for the worst.

CHAPTER 5

Summer school. Talk about two words that do not go together. If someone told me even a month ago that I would be getting up at the crack of dawn to go to the school library to get the forms to sign up for summer school, I would have thought they were auditioning for a commercial for Crazy Town. Yet here I am, walking into the building an hour before classes even start just to get the brochures and registration materials for an encore presentation of Foundations of Science.

We ate another whole cannoli in the park before Ginger was able to convince me that signing up for Foundations of Science in summer school might actually persuade my mother to lift her ban on any and all auditions.

Of course, the library is deserted at this hour of the morning. Even Mrs. Birdsall, the librarian, is still in her office with a cup of coffee and not roaming around like she perpetually does during the school day. I plop my backpack on the table and head toward the back of the room, where the important school forms are kept. As I walk through the stacks, I hear, "Hello, fair maiden. What brings you to this humble reliquary at this hour o' the morn?"

Only one person I know talks like they are a character from a lost chapter of *The Lord of the Rings*, and only one person I know would be in the library before school starts. Nevin Watson. I turn my head and sure enough, I see Nevin's pasty face staring at me.

"Nevin," I say, walking away from him, "don't you ever get tired of doing homework?" Despite the fact that I make sure my tone reflects frustration and annoyance, Nevin takes this as an invitation to follow me around the library.

"Oh, milady, I'm not doing homework. I'm just doing some much-needed personal research related to—"

"That's great, Nevin," I cut him off, hoping to avoid having to hear some boring explanation of wind turbines or Middle-earth mythology or some other dork-infested topic that I have little interest in. I walk farther away from Nevin, and he continues to follow me.

Nevin has had a silly crush on me since forever. He was the first kid I met in our building, and even though he is two years younger than me, he is only one grade behind me because he skipped a year somewhere along the way. I would send Nevin out for any commercial castings that contained the words "nerd," "dork," or "geek." I know that to nerds, dorks, and geeks there is a tremendous amount of difference between each group, but to me they are all the same, and Nevin is their king.

Nevin is actually quite harmless. In fact, when we were little kids, Nevin, Ginger, and I played in the courtyard all the time. When you're little, you just play with whoever happens to be close by. But then I grew out of pretending the fountain was an enchanted castle and that the benches were elves trapped by a spell. I started going out on auditions, where the pretending was much more real. Nevin never quite got the message that I've moved on from childhood games.

After being followed halfway through the library, I finally turn to Nevin and say, "Look, I'm just trying to get some homework done. Can you go back to doing whatever you were doing and I'll just see you around? K?" I try to sound as nice as possible. Nevin is not a bad kid. He's just a bit of a pest.

"Ah, milady needs her private time," Nevin says dramatically as he extends his arm and bows. At least in a few weeks he will be off at math camp or computer camp or whatever camp is the flavor of the month for social misfits. "I cannot tarry myself, as I am here to sign up for summer school. Mr. Rossi said that if I take Foundations of Science this summer, I could take an honors seminar next—"

"What did you say?" I ask. "What did you just say?"

"Tarry?" Nevin asks with a smile. "'Tarry' is an old term. It means—"

"I know what 'tarry' means," I say with an annoyed tone. The truth is, I'm not exactly sure what "tarry" means, but in this moment it could mean purple freaking elephants for all I care. "What did you say about summer school?"

"Just that I am taking it."

"You're taking Foundations of Science this summer?" Nevin just nods his head. He knows I'm in a foul mood, but he can't figure out exactly what he did to put me in my foul mood. I can't believe my luck—or lack thereof. It's one thing to be stuck in summer school, but another to be stuck in summer school with Nevin. He'll be on me like lip gloss on a prom queen. There's no way I could go the whole summer in a class with Nevin without going absolutely insane. Ginger would never make me go through with her plan if she knew that it involved Nevin. On the other hand, Ginger has never understood why he annoys me so much. She finds him perfectly harmless, and at times humorous, which just goes to show you that even Ginger can be wrong.

I am about to turn around and head out of the library, when the thought of being stuck in our crummy apartment all summer flashes through my mind. Ginger will be in Chinese school, and I'll be eating Easy Mac three times a day until I can't fit through the door. The fire department will have to come and cut a hole in the building so I can go back to school in September. Not to mention that I'll have absolutely zero chance of seeing Rory or having my dad see me on TV. I can't let Nevin ruin my life.

This class is the only chance I have, and I'm taking it.

"But Nevin," I say. "You're supposed to take Foundations of Science next year. You're only in sixth grade."

"I know, but if I take it this summer, I can skip seventh-grade science and take eighth-grade science in the fall. Hey, we might even be in the same class next year," Nevin says as a wide smile grows across his face. If only he knew he might not have to wait that long.

CHAPTER 6

After school I make a quick stop at Trinkets, the jewelry shop on Eighth Street next to the bookstore. I know logic and good reason are the primary motivators in my mother's decisions, but I figure a small present might help her have an easier time making a decision in my favor. Everything in the store is a knockoff of the accessories that are sold in fancy department stores, but here the prices are a fraction of what the real things cost. Ginger and I shop here a lot to experiment with trends and see what's current. A month ago we thought these neon feather earrings we started seeing around would hit it big-time, so we came to Trinkets to buy a pair on the cheap. When it turned out they flopped, we didn't feel too bad since we spent only five bucks on one pair that we shared between us. We might have worn them longer if the bright-lime-green peacock feather didn't tickle our necks so much.

It doesn't take me long to find the exact locket that Ashley was wearing at the last audition I had. It's a bubbly heart shape with a lacy design all over it, a small latch on one side, and an even smaller hinge on the other. They come in gold, silver, white, and pink, and they are each only five dollars. I hold the pink one in my hand, since that is the color I would get for myself, but there is no way my mother would wear something so pink. Ashley was wearing the gold one, and I remember her saying that was what all the fake moms were wearing, so that's the one I decide to get.

You would never see any of my mom's jewelry, if you can even call it that, in a commercial. A while ago she went through this crafting period where she made all these pieces from recycled objects. She had a necklace she made from old typewriter keys, a bracelet of bottle caps, and earrings that were once, cringe, Christmas ornaments. She uses the term "repurposed" to describe these creations, but I find them without purpose. This necklace is lovely and will be at least one piece of jewelry that did *not* have a previous life.

The salesgirl wraps the necklace in a fancy gold box and lets me choose the color ribbon I would like. I ask for silver, and she curls the ribbon so it cascades all over the neatly wrapped square.

That night I finish all my homework before dinner in case my mom wants to do a spot check. When I'm done, I place the brochure and course description for summer school that I got from the library on the dining room table next to the wrapped present.

She pulled the plug on my go-sees because of my terrible grade in Foundations of Science. Mrs. Green, the secretary in the guidance office, assured me that if I take the course again over the summer, the new grade will replace the old grade. Since it's only one class and I've already gone through a lot of the material, getting a good grade should take minimum effort. Plus, it meets only two days a week, leaving me plenty of time for auditions. My mom just has to go for this idea.

The thought of calling my dad to rally his support crosses my mind, although I'm not exactly sure what time zone he's in at the moment, so he could be in the middle of something really important or even sleeping. I don't like to think about the fact that he is so far away. In fact, I sort of just pretend he is working a few blocks away, and it usually works. But every now and then I notice his favorite cereal bowl sitting unused in the cabinet or hear the squeak of the bathroom door that he is supposed to fix.

Now that he travels so much, I hardly ever get to see him, but at least he gets to see me, even if it is just for thirty seconds. Also, I can't exactly call him up and tell him that I'm worried he might forget what I look like if he doesn't see me on TV every now and then. I don't want him to feel guilty about the fact that he has to travel so much for work.

I consider cleaning up the kitchen to score some extra points with my mother, but the truth is, the room is a total disaster, and the time I would spend cleaning it would make only the smallest dent in the disarray.

A few months ago I booked a local spot for a bank that was shot on an amazing kitchen set. Everything was spotless and brand-new. There were enough touches on the set, like drawings on the refrigerator and a bowl of dog food next to the door, to make it feel cozy, but not so many as to make the kitchen look messy. I never wanted to leave that kitchen and come back to this one, where the cabinets don't close and the handle on the coffeemaker is held on by some masking tape. The kitchen set was like a daydream or a fairy tale, if fairy tales were set in suburban kitchens instead of castles. Fake sunlight streamed through the fake windows so it looked like a sunny spring morning, even though it was actually snowing outside. It was perfect except for the fact that there were only three walls instead of four, so the cameras could film, and then if you went around the other side of the kitchen, you saw that the walls were basically thick cardboard.

Instead of cleaning the kitchen, I decide to study until my mom comes home. Of course, for most kids this would mean opening a book. For me it means plopping on our lumpy couch and watching TV. I don't check the schedule to see what's on, because I don't care. I'm not watching the programs. Like all the other go-see girls, I'm watching what happens in between the programs. Studying the commercials allows me to stay up on current trends and see who got cast in what. The first commercial I see is for a bank, and while there aren't any girls in it, I have seen the guy playing the teller at a callback. I think his name is Paul. He's short and a little chubby, and he makes these totally hysterical faces. I think he books a lot. When I met him at the callback for an insurance company, he was playing a crossing guard, and he had all the kids cracking up because he was twisting his face into these incredible contortions.

The next commercial starts with the exterior shot of a peaceful suburban house and quickly cuts to the interior. I shout out loud because Ashley, my favorite fake mom, is pretending to dust her house using some new and improved dust cloth. I know this spot, because I got a callback. "Mom, you missed a spot," an off-screen voice says. I totally remember saying that line over and over again in as many different ways as I could. Then I see that Phoebe booked the spot. She looks great, and I love the way she says the line. She's really perfect in it, yet I still get a pang of jealousy seeing her on TV with my favorite fake mom.

The news comes back on, and I shut off the TV, since my mom will be home any second. When I hear her key in the door, I grab the present off the table and run over to greet her. "Hi, Mom," I say, then give her a big hug and hand her the box. "This is for you."

"What's this?" she says, taking the box and pulling off the silver ribbon before opening the lid.

"Oh, it's a necklace," she says. At that moment I notice she is wearing a necklace made out of "repurposed" paper clips. I'm not a moment too soon.

"Actually, it's a locket," I tell her.

"Well, thank you. It's very sweet of you, Cassie," she says, putting the present on the table. "But I must tell you I'm not going to change my mind about the summer unless we can figure out a way to improve your grades."

I step back from my mother and say, "Well, what if I told you I have that all figured out?" I take her hand and walk her to the dining room table, where she sees the materials I have on display.

"Two words, Mom. Summer. School." She takes a seat, and I begin my sales pitch. I emphasize the fact that the new grade will replace my old grade and how having only one class to take will make it easier for me to focus. During this initial pitch, I don't mention commercials at all.

"Well," my mother says, crossing her arms, "I'm very impressed. It looks like you did a lot of research. When does this class meet?"

I take a deep breath and decide to go for the close. "That's the best part," I say, imagining I am at an audition. "It meets early in the morning only twice a week, so I would still have my other days free." Still I do not utter the words, "go-see."

"Mm-hmm," my mother says without opening her mouth. She looks at me suspiciously over the top of her glasses. "And whatever would you do during that free time?" she asks, knowing full well what my answer will be.

"Mom, please. I promise I'll get at least a B. It will be so easy. You said we needed to improve my grade, and this will do it."

My mom gets up from the table, takes the brochure in her hand, and looks at it carefully. I think this is a good sign. She examines the brochure for a few minutes and then looks up at me and says, "A-minus."

I try to show no reaction. She is seriously considering my suggestion. My heart is pounding. I just have to make this work. Now an A-minus would be a total struggle, but I make sure my face doesn't reveal even a trace of panic and say, "B-plus."

My mom thinks for a moment. We stare at each other in silence, and then she says, "Okay. You promise to get a B-plus or better in summer school, and I'll call your agent tomorrow and tell her you're available as soon as summer vacation begins."

I did it. I really did it. I'm so happy I hug my mom, and this time I am truly expressing my genuine affection and joy. I step back from my mom, give her my best commercial smile, and say, "Mom, now that deserves a cheer!"

CHAPTER 7

I'm so excited that I convinced my mother to lift her ban on go-sees that it takes me forever to get to sleep that night. I just stare up at my ceiling in the darkness, picturing myself on the set of some commercial. Cleaning product commercials are the best because the sets are always pristinely clean and the wardrobe is usually conservative and simple. Maybe I'll even book something where Ashley plays my mother. Or maybe I'll book something with Rory. Even having a callback with him would give us an opportunity to hang out more.

After hours of fantasizing, I finally get to sleep at 2:08 a.m. I know the exact time because at 2:09 a.m. my cell phone starts to vibrate. I don't even have to look at the caller ID to know who it is. I swallow hard so it doesn't sound like I just woke up.

"Hi, Dad," I say, loud enough so it doesn't *sound* like I'm trying not to wake up my mom, but quiet enough so I *don't* wake her up.

"Hi, Peanut," my dad says. Peanut is a horrible name that I actually despise, but I've never told my dad that. He likes to call me Peanut, so I just let him. The truth is, I am so excited to hear from him when he calls that he could call me Matilda McGee for all I care. I have gone from seeing my dad every day at every meal to maybe seeing him a few times a month. He always says he's going to take me on the road with him one of these days, but he's been really busy lately, so I just have to wait until things get a little calmer for him.

"I know it's late in New York, Peanut, but I just had to call you. You'll never guess what I just saw."

"What?" I ask.

He tells me how there is this huge flat-screen TV in the lobby of his hotel, and he was with some business friends watching SportsCenter or some kind of sports show on some sports network that I have never heard of. "Well, we're watching the show and they cut to a commercial and BAM! It's my little girl with her face as big as a car."

"Really?" I ask, unable to contain my excitement.

"It was a commercial for some type of security system or something," he says.

"Taylor Trust," I say. "I'm standing outside a white house with blue shutters, and there are two people playing my parents dressed like we're going on a picnic, and there's this huge golden retriever. Right?" I did that shoot almost six months ago. I remember it was the middle of January and freezing outside, but we had to pretend like it was the perfect summer day for a picnic. I was even wearing shorts, and in between takes the wardrobe lady wrapped me in a blanket so I wouldn't freeze to death.

"Yeah, yeah. That's it!" he says. His voice is filled with excitement and pride. It feels great to hear him talk this way. He tells me how he jumped in front of the TV and told everyone that the girl in the commercial was his daughter, Cassie. "It was so cool, Peanut."

I smile to myself and try to stifle a yawn. Even though I am majorly excited that my dad saw me in a spot, it's still two o'clock in the morning and I'm a little groggy. I guess my dad finally picks up on this.

"Oh, jeez, did I wake you up? What time is it there?" he asks.

"Oh, it's not that late," I say. "Where are you?"

"I'm in Palo Alto this week. Look, go back to sleep. I'm sorry I woke you up."

"You didn't wake me up," I lie. "I can't wait to see you next week," I tell him. Seriously, I have been marking the days off on my calendar. Last visit he took me to the Statue of Liberty, and then we had dinner at South Street Seaport. Everything was so perfect it was like being in a commercial. "What time does your flight get in?" I ask.

There is a pause. At first it's a small pause. You almost wouldn't notice it. Then it turns into an actual pause, and when we reach long pause I officially get freaked out because we are moments away from a silence. Then, there it is. We are now officially experiencing a silence, ladies and gentlemen, so please take your seats.

Eventually, "Yeah, about that . . . ," my dad begins, and he doesn't really need to finish for me to know what he's going to say. "Things have been moved around, and I'm not gonna be able to make it next week."

"Oh," is all I say. I don't want to make him feel bad, since I know it isn't his fault. Well, not *exactly* his fault.

"It's late there, and you should go back to bed. If your mom finds out I called so late, she'll have a fit. I'm gonna look at my schedule and we will figure out a visit real soon, okay?"

"That sounds great, Dad," I say, trying to sound excited and happy, but it just doesn't happen. My voice reeks of disappointment.

"Good night, Peanut," he says.

"Good night, Dad," I say, and hang up the phone and slip it back under my pillow.

CHAPTER 8

Usually I mark the countdown until the last day of school in days, but this year I do it in hours. Each morning, before we walk to school, I greet Ginger with, "Three hundred and twenty-two more hours," or whatever number we are at instead of just saying, "Hello" or "Good morning."

The last day of school traditionally marks an ending, but this year it also marks a beginning. After my last class today, my last class for the school year, I will go on my first go-see in twenty-three days. Part of the deal with my mother was that I would finish the school year without distraction. Little did she know that keeping me from auditions proved to be a greater distraction than any booking ever could have been. Since the ban I have thought of nothing else but when the ban will be lifted. Finally, today at three fifteen, after

552 hours, I could possibly go on an audition.

I knock on the door to Ginger's apartment for our walk to school. I'm prepared to say the word "Eight!" and hold up as many fingers, but before I can get the word out of my mouth, the door swings open and Ginger yells, "Eight!" and holds up a blueberry muffin with the number eight on the top made out of blueberries.

We both laugh out loud, and I say, "I don't know who's is going to be happier in eight hours. Me, because the ban is lifted, or you, because you don't have to hear about it anymore."

"Yeah," Ginger says. "That's a tough call. You have been a little obsessed lately, but that's why I wanted to celebrate. My mom and I made these last night. Cute, huh?"

She holds up another muffin, and I pretend to take a bite like I would during an audition and say, "These muffins are eight-zactly what I wanted," using my best commercial voice and smile. Ginger laughs and takes a real bite of her muffin, and I do the same as we walk to the very last day of school.

We sit on the front steps of the school building and finish our muffins, since we're a few minutes early. At first we just chitchat about who looks dorky in the yearbook and what kids are going on cool vacations, and then Ginger says, "I'm thinking about getting a perm."

"What?" I ask as if I didn't hear or something, even though I heard every word.

"A perm. My hair is sooo boring. I need something special. Something a little different," she says, without looking me in the eye. I know exactly what this is about.

"Ginger," I tell her, "your hair is absolutely gorgeous. It's midnight black, perfectly straight and silky. You don't even have a single split end. It's beautiful." It's true Ginger has beautiful hair. Her hair could be on the front of a box of hair dye or on a bottle of shampoo.

"I guess it's okay for hair, but it's so—so—" She stammers for the word for a second. "Boring."

"Your hair is not boring." I search for the exact right phrase. "It's classic." Ginger frowns. She does not want to be classic. We sit in silence for just a few seconds, and then I say, "Does this perhaps have anything to do with the fact that you will be seeing Ming-wei next week?"

"Of course!" Ginger says, throwing her hands in the air. "I mean, this will be the third summer of going to Chinese school, pretending to learn a few hundred new characters while the whole time obsessing over a boy who I'm not sure even knows I'm alive. I just have to do something to have him notice me this summer."

"Well, if you just want to be noticed, we could shave your head entirely. Come by after school today and I'll use one of your dad's razors and make you completely bald. You'll stand out then." I think I'm making a funny joke, but Ginger doesn't laugh.

"I'm not so sure even that would work. Mr. Chu, the director of the school, is bald—and let's not forget Buddha. Ming-wei will probably just rub my tummy and leave me an orange."

Now we both laugh, but my cell phone rings before I can convince Ginger not to do anything drastic.

"It's Honey," I say. "Oh please, please, please let her be calling to tell me I have an audition."

"Well, there's only one way to find out, "Ginger says. "Answer it!"

The last time I talked to Honey she was pulling me from an audition, so I'm a little nervous to answer my phone. I take a deep breath, hope for the best, and say, "Hello?"

CHAPTER 9

When the bell rings to signal the end of the school year, it feels more like a pistol going off at the start of a race than anything else. How many go-sees can I have before the end of the summer? How many spots can I book? How many chances will there be for Dad to see my face popping up on a TV in some airport, and how many opportunities will there be for me to at least come in contact with Rory?

As soon as the bell rings, I bolt down the hall with all the other kids toward the doors, like someone just released all the mice from the biology lab. I pass by Ginger, who is coming out of her final class. She sees me, waves, and shouts, "Break a you know what!" without attempting to delay me. She knows how important this is.

Once I am outside of the school building, I slow

down a bit. I have plenty of time. I just wanted to get out of the building and make the end of school a reality. My summer break is miniscule this year, since I'll be in summer school very soon.

The spot I am auditioning for today is for a new organic cookie called Organica. I'm sure the actual cookie tastes like sawdust, but for the audition I'll have to pretend it tastes like cherry cheesecake. I always use cherry cheesecake as my flavor substitution. Ashley taught me to do that about a year ago when we booked this spot for HealthBits.

The HealthBits shoot was one of the best days I had last year. I auditioned for the spot on a Monday, had the callback on Wednesday, and by Friday I was at the booking. Ashley booked the part of my mom, and it was the second time we played mother and daughter.

I loved the HealthBits set so much I wanted to live in it. A large, modern suburban kitchen with sunlight streaming through the windows. Every detail was polished and perfectly placed, yet it still felt homey. I took a picture of the set with my camera phone and for a while I used it as my screen saver. Of course, this perfect kitchen was in the middle of a huge soundstage in the warehouse district of Queens, but the way I cropped my photo you would never know.

In the scene Ashley and I had to devour a plate of HealthBits, a snack so vile and disgusting that stray dogs would turn away from it. Ashley read the list of ingredients from the package and found out that they contained chocolate (yeah!) and seaweed (yuck!). Ashley told me to just imagine that each HealthBit was a piece of cherry cheesecake. Since cherry cheesecake is an unusual flavor, it meant my facial expression would move from curiosity to pleasure to satisfaction, which is what most commercials want. I did that, and the director loved how we worked together. Unfortunately, I never saw the finished spot because HealthBits never made it to the general public. They went out of business just after we filmed the commercial.

I press the elevator button for the seventeenth floor and wait for the ancient elevator to make its way up the building. I'm glad my first go-see of the season is at Betsy Barnes Casting. They cast a lot of kids, so chances are a lot of my friends will be there. That is one thing I love about go-sees. You never know what's going to happen.

I get off the elevator, follow the arrow to the

right, and see Millie sitting behind the sign-in desk.

"Hey, it's been a few weeks since I've seen you. Has the ban finally been lifted?" Millie asks as she hands me a clipboard and I start filling out my information.

"Does everyone know I was grounded?" I ask.

"Well, Julie told Timmy, and Timmy told—"

"Millie, you don't have to finish that sentence. If Timmy told anyone, then he told everyone."

"Yeah, that's how he operates. Sorry," she says, smiling a bit. I'm not upset that Timmy blabbed about me being gone. I actually kind of like the fact that he did. It means on some level I was missed, and it's always nice to be missed. I hand my materials to Millie and go down the hall and wait to be called in.

I open the door to the studio, and Faith is sitting in a chair looking at the storyboard for the spot. Faith prepares meticulously for each audition. She doesn't allow even a hair out of place before she goes into the studio. I'm much more casual with it all.

There are a few other girls in the studio, but I don't recognize any of them. I can tell by looking around the room that the casting call was not very specific. It must have said something like "all tween girls" because even though all the girls are about the same age and have the same commercial "look," no one type is in the room. Sometimes they want all sporty blondes or all geeky redheads so when you walk in a room it's like looking into a hall of mirrors. Today there is a lot more variety. I also notice that most of the girls are on their own. Even last year the room was filled with moms or guardians. I went out on my own a lot earlier than many of the other kids, since I was born and raised in the city.

The door to the studio opens, and a very pretty Indian girl about my age walks out. Vicky Chow, who must be running the casting session, pops out behind her, looking at her clipboard.

"Okay, Faith. You're next."

Faith looks a little nervous, like she's not ready. She opens her purse and says, "Can I wait, Vicky? My mom is calling me." She takes out her phone, which doesn't seem to be vibrating at all. I guess it's on some total silence setting. "Can you take someone else?" she asks, and turns to look at me.

"I haven't really had a chance to look at the sides," I say.

I look at Vicky, who shrugs.

"Sure, I'll go in," I say. Maybe helping Faith out will make her a little less tense and competitive.

I follow Vicky into the studio and start picturing a mouthwatering slice of cheesecake covered in bright red cherries.

CHAPTER 10

Vicky Chow is new at Betsy Barnes Casting. She is sweet but is one of those casting directors who treat the kids like kids. There is nothing wrong with that, I suppose, since we are, after all, kids, but still there are other casting offices where we are treated just like the adults.

Vicky asks me how school is and if I have any big plans for summer as she sets up the camera and explains the spot to me. I get the feeling she has asked the same questions to every girl who has come in here, so I just give her the answers I think she wants to hear.

School is fine. I'll hang out with my friends this summer.

I slate by saying my name and my agency directly to the camera. "I'm Cassie Herold and I'm with Honey's Kids." We run through the spot twice. She gives me the simple adjustment to go a bit slower. I take a deep breath. I do the spot a second time and try not to behave like a roller coaster without brakes. Vicky grabs her clipboard and puts a check next to my name.

I walk out of the studio with Vicky, and Millie is waiting for her. "Vick, can you help us with a tech issue in Studio Three?"

"Sure, Millie. Girls, I'll be back in a minute. Faith, you're next." Vicky rushes out of the waiting room to fix whatever the problem could be.

"Is everything all right with your mom?" I ask Faith. She looks at me kind of funny.

"My mom? Oh yeah, my mom. Yeah, everything is fine. Thanks for going in for me."

"Sure, no problem," I say. Faith smiles but goes back to studying the copy. I look around the room to see if there is anybody else I know, but I don't really recognize anyone. Well, I actually recognize a few of the girls from spots they've booked but I don't actually know them. It's weird how seeing someone on television makes you feel like you know them, even though you have never met.

Vicky comes back into the room. She smooths down her already smooth black bob and says, "I'm glad I have you girls today. Studio One is a spot for a new video game. The place is wall-to-wall boys. I don't know how Timmy is going to make it through the day."

Wall-to-wall boys? That means Rory might be in Studio One.

"Faith, come on in," Vicky says, opening the door.

Faith puts her copy on the chair and reluctantly follows Vicky into the studio.

I walk out of the studio and down the hall to Studio One. There's no harm in just walking by and looking through the window to see if Rory is in there. It's not in the direction of the elevator, but still I could just pretend I was lost. The hallway is empty, so I walk very slowly past the door. The window in the door is just a bit too high for me to see anything at all. I can, however, hear the unmistakable rumble of boys. Since the hallway is still empty, I walk past again, but still I can't see anything. The elevator opens, and a boy about my age in a Little League outfit walks out with his mom behind him. I figure this might be an opportunity.

I kneel down and pretend I'm tying my shoe and wait for my chance. The boy and his mom pick up a size card quickly and walk over to the studio, and as soon as they open the door I get up and just sort of join them without their knowing and walk into Studio One.

Once inside I realize I needn't have worried about anyone noticing me. The waiting area is packed with kids and parents and their sibs and friends. I could have walked in dressed as Little Bo Peep and no one would have noticed. I decide to use this to my advantage. I casually walk over to the sign-in sheet, where everyone auditioning has to put their name, agency, and call time. I figure if Rory has already been here, there is no chance of running into him. I look down the list and even turn it over to see if he was in any of the morning spots. Nothing. Then I check to see if his agency, Theory, has had any of the slots. No one from Theory has signed in, so that means if Rory has gotten an appointment for this spot, it's not until later.

I could simply wait here and blend in with the crowd, but what will I do when and if he shows up? How will I explain myself? I panic a bit thinking about being found in this waiting room, where I might be able to blend in but obviously don't belong. I walk out of the room quickly and feel a sense of relief once I am back in the hall.

I push the button and wait for the elevator. I

can't believe I was so close to running into Rory on my first day back to go-sees. I could hang out in the hall or outside the building, but that would be too obvious. I get into the elevator and take out my phone to text Ginger. I know she'll want an immediate update. I start punching in the letters on my cell as the elevator makes its slow descent. The doors open and I'm still working on my message, so I walk out without looking up from the screen and run right into Rory.

As soon as I realize what I've done, I'm mortified. I try to cover it up by just playing it cool. "Oh, hey, Rory. How have you been?" I think about apologizing for running smack-dab into him but figure it's better to admit nothing.

Rory looks a little confused, and I can't tell if it's because I just walked into him or some other reason. The truth is, we barely know each other. I first saw Rory on a commercial for a candy bar, where he's on a date with a girl. The commercial shows them going to a movie, and then they hold hands walking home and share a candy bar. That commercial has got to be the most romantic thirty seconds ever put on film. I probably saw that commercial a few dozen times, and somewhere around the twentieth viewing I solidified my crush on Rory. So what if we had not actually met at that point? Then about a year ago, we were part of the same crowd scene in a soap commercial.

There were so many kids there it was hard to really spend any time with Rory, but I stood next to him in line for lunch, and he introduced himself and asked me if they had any more peanut butter granola bars. Not exactly *Wuthering Heights*, but it was a start.

Since that booking I have been seeing him around at auditions but haven't actually spoken to him. But it looks like that is about to change. Finally he opens his mouth, and I realize we are going to actually have some sort of conversation or something. This is way beyond a silent wave from across the room.

"What's up, Monique?" he says, and flashes his toothpaste-commercial-worthy smile at me. For a second, I melt. I mean, that smile alone is enough to make a girl faint right there in the lobby.

I raise my hand up from my side and wiggle my fingers in what I hope resembles a wave. The elevator doors close as I stare and do my strange finger wave. Once the doors shut it's like a spell has been broken, and I am transported back to reality.

"Monique? Monique! Did he just call me Monique?" I look around the lobby as if searching for a witness to this terrible turn of events. I was so caught up in just being in his presence that I failed to realize that he called me by an entirely different name. I could almost understand it as a mistake if he'd called me something even remotely related to my name, but it's not like he called me Cathy or Katie or even Sassy or Lassie. He called me *Monique*, and I didn't even say anything. I was so focused on the fact that he was talking to me that I failed to listen to what he was actually saying.

I thought the worst thing in the world would be not running into Rory at all. Boy, was I wrong.

CHAPTER 11

"*My cousins in Toronto had a poodle named Monique.*
They tried to put pink bows in her hair, but she kept
eating them and throwing them up," Ginger tells me
as we walk out of our apartment building.

"Ginger, that's disgusting, not to mention far
from comforting," I tell her. We are walking to our
respective summer schools. Honestly, I can't be too
mad at Ginger for her poodle story. I have told her
the elevator mortification moment so many times
that even I am at a loss to find a new angle on the
subject. When we get to school, we sit on the steps,
since we have some time before I have to face the
first day of summer classes.

"Look, at least Rory knows you're alive. Granted,
he may in fact have you confused with someone
else, but that's a good sign. I mean, the fact that he
knows you are alive. I'm about to go to my third

year of Chinese school with Ming-wei, and he doesn't even know I exist, so the way I see it, you're way ahead of me."

She's right. Ginger has been going to the same school with Ming-wei for years, and he has never even acknowledged her presence. "Ginger, this is the year we are going to change that. If nothing else, you are going to talk to Ming-wei."

Ginger shakes her head frantically. "No," she says. "There is no way I could just go up to him and"—she swallows hard, like she's is trying to get down a particularly revolting piece of meat loaf—"and talk to him."

"Well," I tell her, "maybe we could think of something to get him to talk to you."

Ginger scrunches up her face, looks at her hands, and then holds them up to me. "Look, I'm already sweating just thinking about it." Ginger has an issue with her palms sweating when she is nervous. "You better go to class. You don't want to be late for the first day," she says.

"Don't change the subject. You should—"

"Well, if it isn't two fair maidens on the steps of ye old school building," Nevin says, interrupting me.

"Hi, Nevin," we both say almost in unison,

although Ginger's tone is not anywhere near as annoyed as mine. I had almost forgotten that Nevin would be in my summer class. I guess that's what they call denial.

"I better get downtown. I'll see you guys later," Ginger says, getting up from the steps.

"Bye, Ginger," I say.

"*Zàijiàn* Wen-Ying. *Zàijiàn*," Nevin says, and then turns to me. "I was only saying good-bye in the young lady's native tongue using her Chinese name." This makes Ginger smile for some reason, and she waves good-bye and heads down the block. I give Nevin a look as if to say, *Can't you just a be a little normal?*

I walk into the building and don't even have to look behind me to know that Nevin has followed me in.

"Do you think we'll be able to use our own scientific calculators for class or will they only allow standard calculators?"

"Nevin, what in the world is a scientific calculator? A calculator is just a calculator, and who cares?"

"Actually, calculators are fascinating little machines, and scientific calculators vary a great deal in terms of . . ."

For a second I think about cutting Nevin off but realize it would only prompt him to start in on some other inane topic. Best let him run out of gas on this calculator thing and just tune him out as we take our seats.

My plan is to be super organized for this summer class. Of course, this is my plan at the start of *every* school year, but something happens around the second or third week. My foolproof plan for academic success gets off track, and before I know it I've missed a homework assignment or forgotten to study for a quiz or I'm so bored by class that I've totally zoned out most of the material. Not this summer. This summer I'm going to be prepared. A bad grade in this class could mean the end of commercials forever, and I am not about to let that happen. I will do whatever it takes.

"Good morning, everyone. I am Mr. Evans, and I will be your teacher for Foundations of Science this summer. Instead of starting at the beginning, I would like to start at the end."

Oh, great. Three seconds into class and I'm already confused. What does he mean, start at the end?

"I'd like to tell you about your final exam for

class." A couple of kids groan quietly, and I'd join their chorus if I had a better idea of what the teacher was talking about. "I know no one likes to take a final exam and especially for a summer class, so your final exam will be held during the last class at the City Science Center and Museum, where you will work in teams to use the scientific principles we will cover this summer to do a variety of experiments."

This announcement gets a favorable reaction from most kids, but I am reluctant to approve. A final exam is still a final exam. It doesn't matter where it takes place. Still, it's better than sweating over a page covered in small ovals waiting to be filled in with the correct answer to some torturous multiple-choice question.

"You should have on your desk a copy of the textbook we will be using," Mr. Evans continues. "Will you please turn to the first page of chapter one on 'Scientific Inquiry'?"

I quickly open my book and find the page. Once I have it, I take a good look at Mr. Evans. He seems like a nice enough guy. He has wavy black hair that looks like he just combed it and a wrinkled forehead that makes him look like he is always in deep thought. If I were to send him out on a casting it would be for the role of a doctor for some type of aspirin or pain medication. He has a warm, open smile, and it makes me think he will be an easy grader. At least, I hope he will be.

"We are going to start right in looking at the process of scientific inquiry. Will someone begin reading from the first sentence here on page eight?" he asks. One of the girls raises her hand and starts reading. I hate reading aloud in class. It's one thing to read the script at an audition, but reading aloud in class always makes me nervous. Last year in my social studies class I had to read an article on political leaders in the Middle East out loud, and I mispronounced one of the names so badly it sounded like a word commonly used to describe something terrible that can happen to you in a bathroom. It was humiliating, so I try to avoid reading aloud in class whenever I can.

I turn to a fresh page in my notebook and prepare to take notes, when I feel my phone vibrate. It's too early for Honey to be calling me for an audition, and Ginger is in Chinese school.

I make sure Mr. Evans is not looking at me and very carefully turn the phone over to see the screen. It's my dad. I take in a quick breath, which catches Mr. Evans's attention. I cough politely to cover my excitement, and Mr. Evans goes back to reading along in his textbook.

I haven't spoken to my dad in days. I know he's been really busy with work, so this may be the only window I have to actually hear his voice. I decide to turn my polite cough into a larger distraction so I can talk to my dad. I start with a small, simple clearing of the throat that you might use to get someone's attention and then move into a full-blown cough syrup commercial cough, like I have just swallowed a hair ball. Then I go all out with a cough that sounds like I've swallowed a cat that has swallowed a hair ball.

Mr. Evans can no longer ignore my interruption. "Miss, do you need to use the restroom or get a drink of water?" He walks over to me and hands me the hall pass. I nod while still coughing and quietly move my cell phone from my bag to my pants pocket. I grab the pass and head out of the classroom.

Since it's summer, the building is quiet, like a church on a Wednesday afternoon—the spirit is still there but the congregation is somewhere else. I walk to the back stairwell, where I know I will be able to have some privacy, and hit the callback button on my phone.

"Michael Herold," I hear my dad say. He always answers the phone using his full name, since he never knows if it might be a business call.

"Hi, Dad, it's me. I think you just called me, but I was coming out of the subway so the reception was bad." I don't like to lie, but I don't want him to feel bad about interrupting me during class.

"How's my favorite girl? How's my Peanut?" he asks. His voice is warm and easy. My dad could be the announcer in a luxury automobile commercial. "Book any big spots I should start looking for?"

I wish I could say yes. I wish I was about to appear on a TV near him any moment now, but I just started back, so it might be a few weeks until I book anything at all. "Not yet, Dad," I say. "But I did have a go-see just the other day."

"Good for you." He clears his throat. "Uh, Cassie, there's been a change of plans. . . ." My father says this a lot. He changes plans more often than most people change socks.

I try to prepare myself not to get too disappointed. "Yeah?" I say as evenly as possible.

"I know I was scheduled to come and see you in two weeks, right?" he starts. Actually, twelve days and fourteen hours, but who's counting? "Well, I'm not going to make it," he says. I feel my face start to get red. I cannot go back to class with tears in my eyes. I squeeze my eyelids tightly.

"I'm actually flying into New York this Friday. Is that all right?"

My eyes pop open, and any thought of tears flies out of my head. "This weekend? Like, in four days? Are you serious? Oh, Daddy, that's great. That's fantastic. I can't wait."

I can hear him chuckling on the other end of the phone. My dad has this great deep chuckle that you wish you could bottle and open whenever you were having a bad day. "Look," he says, "I've got to get on this flight to Tampa, but I'll call your mom and make sure it's all right with her. Love you, Cas. See you soon."

"You too, Dad. Bye," I say, and hang up the phone.

This time I actually turn off my cell phone. I walk back to class, and Mr. Evans is writing something on the board about scientific inquiry that already doesn't make sense to me. It's only the first day of class and I'm already behind, but it doesn't matter because I feel like I'm ahead.

CHAPTER 12

I swear I answer 90 percent of my mom's questions with the same word. "How was school?" Fine. "How was the callback?" Fine. "How do you feel about having lasagna for dinner?" Fine. "What's a word that rhymes with line?" Fine. However, my unchanging response doesn't stop her from asking me a thousand questions every chance she gets. I love my mom, but sometimes I wonder how we are related. She loves mathematics and crafting, and I like hanging out with my friends and going on auditions. We could not be more different.

When I was little, I used to love coming to her office on campus. It seemed like such a magical place, but now, as I stare at my soggy tuna-and-sprouts sandwich, her office seems about as appealing as my lunch. When she asked me to have lunch with her, I was hoping that would mean some sunny sidewalk café where I could people watch and look out for cute boys.

"And how do you like Mr. Evans?" my mom asks.

The word "fine" just rolls out of my mouth, but I can tell my mom is trying hard to make conversation, so I dig just a bit deeper. "I mean, he seems like a nice guy. He's not too old, and so far he hasn't given us too much homework." I take a final bite of my soggy sandwich before covering it with paper. "But I forgot to tell you the worst part of class."

"What's that?" my mom asks. I can tell she's excited that I'm sharing something without her prodding.

"Nevin!" I announce.

"Is Nevin in your class? But he's younger than you are."

"I know, right? He's taking it for extra credit or something stupid like that. Can you believe it? Extra credit? Over the summer?"

My mom takes a bite of her sandwich and then smiles with her mouth closed for a second. "I know Nevin can be a bit of a pest, but he's not a bad kid. You know he worships you. Just be nice to him."

"I am," I say quickly, not sure if I'm being honest.

"When you were little, you and Ginger *and* Nevin

were together all the time. The three of you would play in the courtyard until it got dark. You and Ginger even spent a couple of summers with Nevin's family at the beach house on the Jersey shore. Remember?"

"I remember," I say. It's true that when we were kids the three of us hung out, but as we got older, we hung out less. Part of it had to do with the fact that girls and boys generally stopped hanging out together, and part of it has to do with the fact that Nevin got deeply into his dork stage. I'm still hoping to put as much distance between my dork stage and whatever stage it is I'm in now. Still, it's weird to remember that we used to hang out so much when we were younger.

"Just remember, Cassie. Sometimes when you kiss a frog, he turns out to be a prince."

"Mom, please! I'm eating." The very thought of kissing Nevin or that he might actually turn out to be a prince is disgusting. I glance at the clock behind her and see that it's almost one. I shove what's left of my lunch in my paper bag and put it in my backpack. "I better go to my audition or else I'll be late."

My mom sighs. "Well, at least these things are teaching you a good work ethic. Have fun," she says. I give her a kiss good-bye and I'm out the door.

CHAPTER 13

The waiting room at Betsy Barnes Casting is packed.
I knew it would be. There are two distinct groups waiting outside the studio. All the girls are huddled together on one side, and the boys are hanging out on the other side of the room. It's only recently that we started dividing this way. A few years ago all the boys and girls just hung out together. I go to the sign-in and grab the sides from the assistant so I can see if there are any lines I need to memorize. Before I even look at the sides or write down my name, I scan the sign-in sheet to see if RR is here.

"Yes!" I say out loud when I see his name on the list just a few spaces above mine. Even his handwriting is cute. It's sloppy but in a very bold sort of way. I sign my name as girly as possible with big, loose loops in case Rory decides to look over the names to see if I'm here. Once I sign in, I remember that he thinks my name is Monique, so I guess it doesn't matter how I sign my name.

I grab the sides and go over the storyboard. It's a "vignette" spot, which means they're going to film a bunch of scenes and put them together. The fun part about this type of commercial is that you get to be in lots of different shots. The bad part is that they shoot so many different scenes that not all of them make it into the final cut of the commercial. I shot a vignette spot for a cat food a year ago, and my face never made it to the actual commercial. I think that bothers some kids but not me. I try to focus on the storyboard in front of me, when I suddenly see HIM out of the corner of my eye.

At first I'm excited, but then I quickly remember that he doesn't know my name. He thinks I'm *Monique.* I can't exactly go over to him and say hello when he doesn't know my name. I could reintroduce myself and tell him my name, but that's pretty bold even for me. I decide to position myself across from him on the other side of the room and engross myself in the copy. That way I will be far enough away so he won't actually have to talk to me, but close enough so he'll see me and I can smile or wave. Maybe even smile *and* wave.

The studio door opens, and four kids walk out. The casting assistant compares the sign-in sheet with her clipboard and announces a list of names to go in next. She ends with, ". . . and Rory Roberts. In now, please."

Rory gets up, and as he begins to walk toward the studio he sees me. I decide to cut the wave and just smile. He sees me, smiles back, and gives me a sort of half wave, which is a lot for a boy. His smile alone would have been enough for me, but the half wave is the icing on my cake. So what if he doesn't know my name? What's the big deal with a name? He knows who I am, and that's what's important. I smile to myself, knowing I've accomplished at least half of what I have set out to do today.

I pick up the sides again and begin to study each panel. Sure, seeing RR is a highlight, but booking the spot is what I am here to do. If I totally mess up my go-see, that means no callback, and no callback means no booking, and no booking means no chance of my dad seeing me on TV, and that means I am basically wasting my time in summer school. The spot seems easy enough, so I just think of some facial expressions that would work for each scene.

Rory's group comes out, and I pretend I am

deeply engrossed in the sides. We've already had a moment today, so I don't want to push it. I should probably try to start a conversation with him or something, but we already had the wave, and I'm not sure I want to deal with the whole Monique thing. I hide behind my pages and carefully watch as he walks down the hall and out of sight. He's wearing a royal blue polo that reminds me of a print ad he was in for a fast-food restaurant, where he's with his family, enjoying a meal of cheeseburgers and shakes. He wore a blue polo shirt and his usual incredible smile. I know the ad well, because I had it hanging in my locker all last year.

Another group goes in and comes out and then I'm finally called in. The casting director goes over the scene. It's pretty simple. We're just a bunch of kids hanging out at an amusement park. During the day, the group of girls keeps running into the group of boys, and one of the boys starts to like one of the girls, and romance blossoms.

We each slate, and then everyone alternates playing the friend or part of the couple. I get distracted for a bit when I realize that just a few minutes ago Rory was in this room pretending to be someone's boyfriend. I would do anything to have him pretend to be my boyfriend. Then I confuse myself, because I would like him to be my real boyfriend, but in a way, the pretend image is so much nicer.

I try to focus on the audition. It's a bit hard pretending the messy room is an amusement park, but I do my best to imagine the feel of the summer sun, the smell of freshly spun cotton candy, and the sound of muffled screams going down the steepest hill of the roller coaster. We run through each scene a few times, and then the casting director says she has what she needs on tape and we leave the studio. The amusement park that I created in my head melts away like an ice cube thrown in a fire.

As I walk out of the studio I see Phoebe and her brother Liam. I'm not surprised, since everyone wants to book Phoebe lately. I bet she would be perfect for the girlfriend role in this spot. "Hey, guys," I say. I know her brother goes with her just to help her out, which is incredibly sweet. Still I ask, "Are you both here to audition for the spot?"

"Please, like Liam would ever get in front of the camera," Phoebe says. She laughs and moves her long blond hair from one shoulder to the other.

"No, thank you. I'm strictly a behind-the-camera kind of guy," Liam says. The truth is, Liam is a really cute boy and would do very well. As a matter of fact, he was on my Crush List a few months ago, but he is way too much of a rebel to really have any chance of moving into my top three. Rory has a bit more charm, in my opinion, and a bit more mystery. Also, Liam and I are friends, so if there had been a romantic spark I'd know by now.

I hang out with Phoebe and Liam for a little while, since I don't have to be home right away and Phoebe is pretty far down on the list to go in. She tells me that she just shot another ad for Pizza Fantastic a week or so ago. Phoebe has been booking like crazy ever since her brother started going out with her on auditions. She says he's her good luck charm.

"Oh, hey," Phoebe says, all excited. "Why don't you come out to Great Neck this weekend? They're opening the pool at the swim club, and it's supposed to be a scorcher. You could take the train and we could play volleyball with the other kids at the club."

Liam, who has been drawing with a pencil on a pad about the size of his lap, looks up. "Yeah, Cassie, you should come out to Long Island this weekend. We could go to that ice cream place again. I'm sure that schnauzer has forgiven you."

"Will I ever live that down?" I ask, and they both laugh. The last time I visited them, we got ice cream cones at Scoops. We walked out of the store, and I went to take my first lick, but the ice cream was not firmly on the cone, so my tongue accidentally pushed it off its base. It landed smack-dab on a miniature schnauzer, who did not seem too happy about being covered in mint chocolate chip ice cream. We offered to wash the dog for the owner, but I think he just wanted to get away from us, and so did the dog. Thinking about it still cracks me up.

"Guys, I would love to come out there. It sounds totally amazing," I tell them, "but I actually have plans this weekend."

Phoebe gasps. "Do you have a date with you-know-who?"

"Who is you-know-who?" I ask, pretending not to know she is talking about Rory.

"Please. Everyone in this room knows who you-know-who is. I mean, I don't officially know who you-know-who is, and even I know who you-know-who is." Liam's sentence sounds so ridiculous that the three of us laugh out loud, and Phoebe hits Liam on the arm.

"Liam, be nice," she says. "Don't worry. We know

who you mean because we're your friends, but no one else has any idea. Liam is just being Liam."

"Phew," I say. "Anyway, it doesn't matter, because he's *not* the guy I'm seeing this weekend."

"Well, from the sound of your voice, it seems like it's someone pretty special," Phoebe says.

"It is," I say. "It's my dad!"

CHAPTER 14

I get up at the crack of dawn on the day I'm supposed to see my dad. Okay, it's actually eight thirty, but on a Saturday, it feels like the crack of dawn. My plan is to spend some time cleaning my room and then do the breakfast dishes. I try to be extra nice to my mom on the days when my dad is in town. I wish she would just come with us, but she says since my dad is away so much, it's important for the two of us to spend time alone together. I've tried to convince her that it's more fun when all three of us are together, but she won't budge. It's been so long since the three of us were together in the same place at the same time that maybe whatever problems made it difficult for us to all be together have sort of just disappeared.

I walk out of my room, and the rest of the apartment smells like pancakes and syrup. My mom is sitting at the kitchen counter finishing her granola and soy milk. "Oh, good, you're up," she says. "I made pancakes and waffles, so you can have your choice, or you can have both. And I didn't put any wheat germ or fiber flakes or natural anything in them. Here, I even bought this." She hands me an unopened bottle of Southern Charm Pancake Syrup, the kind that is supersweet and has only a very casual relationship to maple syrup.

"Wow!" I say. My mom knows how much I dislike her organic, all natural, looks–like–tree–bark–and–tastes–like–tree–bark healthy food. Of course, maple syrup is one thing that I don't mind, but I don't tell her that. "Thanks, Mom. This looks great." When I look at the spread she has created and think about how I just spent the last hour cleaning my room in order to make her happy, I consider how we are more alike than I think.

But then when I look at my mom, I realize how different we are. She's wearing the same pair of sweatpants she has worn for years, and her SAVE THE WILDLIFE T-shirt, which is so old it has faded from bright red to dull pink. At least she's wearing the locket I gave her. In fact, the day after I gave it to her she put a picture of me as a baby in it. The gold heart looks nice even against her less-than-fashionable T-shirt.

She undoes her braid on the weekends, so today her gray-and-brown hair looks wild and unruly. I think about Ashley's short, layered cut and how chic and modern it looks.

"Do you ever think about cutting your hair?" I ask as matter-of-factly as possible, like I just asked her to pass the salt or something.

"Well, Mona just gave me a trim the other day," she says, unaware of the real intention behind my question. Mona is the administrative aide in my mom's office, and she cuts my mom's hair because she happened to move into an apartment where someone left behind one of those salon chairs that goes up and down. Mona is getting her degree in statistics and knows absolutely nothing about cutting hair.

"Mom, Mona is not a stylist. You said yourself she uses those kindergarten scissors with the round edges."

My mom pats her hair down a bit, "Well, those seem to work just fine, and it doesn't cost me a penny."

The intercom buzzes, and my mom bristles. "Well, that must be your dad," she says stiffly.

"Why is he buzzing the apartment and not just using his key to come up?" I ask. If I am being honest with myself, I might actually know the answer to this question, but my mom answers before I can think about it too much.

"Well, I'm sure he just wants to spend as much time with you as possible," she says, opening the door for me.

"Don't you want to see him?" I ask.

My mom hesitates and shakes her head a bit, like she doesn't know what to say. Then finally, "Oh, it's such a short visit. Let's not waste any of it."

I decide to push this just a bit. "C'mon, just come down with me." I know they have been having problems lately, but I figure this is just due to the fact that they haven't seen each other in a while. Maybe if my mom came down she would see that Dad is not such a bad guy. I know they have different opinions about things, but still, we're a family, and we should do things together. After all, the whole idea of a trial separation is that you are just giving it a try. That means you should also give *being together* a try. Why am I the only person in this family who is able to see that?

"No, Cassie. I think it's better if you just run down. Do you have your cell phone? Money in your wallet? Are you wearing sunscreen?" The questions come at me in rapid succession as my mom walks to the door and opens it for me. I answer yes to everything, tell her I love her, and head out the door to meet my dad.

"Dad!" I scream when I spot him outside the lobby of our building. My dad looks perfect. He's wearing a light green polo top and khaki shorts. He could be cast right now as the dad in a commercial that takes place during a family picnic or a weekend getaway. I wrap my arms around his chest and hug him tightly, but I can't help thinking how much better this would be if we were all together like a real family.

By three o'clock I am exhausted and a little nauseous. We have been to the Central Park Zoo, the Metropolitan Museum of Art, and Bloomingdale's. I've eaten popcorn, a hot dog with ketchup and sauerkraut, cotton candy, a pretzel with mustard, an ice cream bar, and half a bottle of water. If there was a street cart selling it, my dad bought it, and I ate it.

For the first time since we left the apartment this morning, we are sitting down, and it feels good. We found a quiet bench under a tree, and now that we've been sitting for a few minutes, I'm not sure I will ever be able to get up.

At first just being still and quiet feels good, but after a few minutes it gets a little uncomfortable. We've been so busy doing stuff all day that we haven't really had time to just sit and be together. It's weird having him on the road, because when I spend time with him, it feels like we're always trying to squeeze in all this quality time into just a few hours. The truth is, I don't want quality time, I just want regular old hanging-out-not-doing-much-of-anything time. I don't know who invented quality time, but they sure got it wrong.

We sit in silence for a few more minutes, but the distance grows uncomfortable, and I start racking my brain, trying to think of things to say or something to ask my dad. I could ask him why he's traveling so much and why Mom won't come downstairs to see him when he's in town. He'd tell me the answer if I just ask him, but the truth is, I don't want to know.

Finally my dad breaks the silence. "Hey, did I tell you that I saw your commercial for that security company again?"

"Really?" I say.

"Yeah, this time I was just in my hotel room getting ready for a meeting, and I had the news on or something, and then all of a sudden, bam, there was my girl." My dad's face lights up when he talks about seeing me on TV. "Have you booked anything recently?"

"Uh, no . . . ," I say. He knows I've been grounded for the past month or so, but I guess he forgot. "But I did have a great audition the other day for an amusement park. Maybe I'll get a callback and book that. It's a national. I'm sure you would see it in one of your hotels."

"That would be great," he says, and I smile at him. It's weird thinking of him seeing me when he's thousands of miles away, but here I am, sitting a few inches from him, and I wonder if he sees me at all. I get a pit in my stomach and think about my last go-see. I hope I did good enough to get a callback. I'd really love to have my dad see me in that spot.

"Hey," my dad says. "You know what we haven't done yet? We haven't gone on the carousel. C'mon, let's go take a ride or even a few."

The carousel? Does he have any idea how much I have eaten in the past few hours? Taking me on the carousel is just asking for trouble. My stomach rumbles at the very thought of spinning around in circles while grabbing on to a brightly painted wooded horse, praying I won't toss my cookies. I don't tell my dad any of this. Instead I just pretend I am in the middle of a shoot for a commercial. I smile, hop up from the bench, and say, "That sounds great. Let's go."

CHAPTER 15

Ginger is full of questions on Monday morning as we walk to our schools. With my dad in town, I wasn't able to see her for almost two full days. We barely go more than two full hours without speaking, so two days feels like forever. She wants to know every detail of every minute I spent with my dad. It's nice to have a best friend who is so interested in your life, but the truth is, there isn't much to tell.

"It was just a nice weekend," I tell her, and shrug. I don't tell her that sometimes it's hard to talk to my dad or that sometimes I want him to talk to me more. I don't tell her about how guilty I feel when I'm with my dad, because I know it means my mom is at home alone, or worse, in her office working on some math equation. Ginger knows I adore my dad, and I don't want her thinking anything otherwise. I try to change the subject and ask Ginger about her weekend out of the city with her parents. "How was Provincetown?" I ask.

"The weather was great, and we got to use that wheelchair with the super-huge wheels so it can go in the sand. That was fun, but my parents made us go to this poetry reading for one of their friends. And I swear it's, like, impossible for my parents to pass a used bookstore without going in. I mean, seriously, how many copies of *Leaves of Grass* can they own?" Ginger's parents have an incredible collection of books by Walt Whitman, a poet that her mom really admires. I think the collection is cool, since most of the books in our house have numbers and math symbols on every page. I'd love to have books on our shelves with titles I understand.

We get to the front of the school building and I say, "Hey, you know what? Let's make grilled cheeses after classes today. Like we did last summer." Last summer we made grilled cheeses for lunch almost every day, and we never got sick of them.

"That's a great idea," Ginger says. "I think we have everything we need at my place, but I'll just text my parents and make sure."

Then I decide to make things more interesting. "And let's make a deal," I say.

"I don't like the sound of this." Ginger looks at me with concern.

"I'll do all the dishes, if you talk to Ming-wei."

Ginger stops dead in her tracks. "You mean actually talk to him. Like using . . . words and stuff."

"Yes," I tell her. "Using words and stuff. You can do it. It's now or never." I take her by the shoulders and point her in the direction of her school. "Be brave, my friend, and look on the bright side. You can speak to him in English or Chinese. You have two whole languages to choose from." I give her a gentle push toward her destiny and say good-bye.

I have a few minutes before class starts, so I use the time to sit in the sun with my eyes closed and just chill before being stuck inside. I've barely closed my eyes when I feel my cell phone start to vibrate. I assume it's Ginger, since she often calls me two minutes after seeing me to tell me something incredibly important that she's forgotten.

I take out my cell phone and see that it isn't Ginger, it's my agent.

My heart skips a beat. Could this be about getting a callback for the Seven Sails amusement park spot? Maybe it's another audition for something else.

"Hello?" I say.

"Hi, Cassie. It's Honey, and I have a callback for you for the Seven Sails spot this afternoon."

"Fantastic!" I shout.

"Well, just keep your grades up, Cassie. I've heard through the grapevine that there are some major campaigns coming up at the end of the summer."

"I will," I say, and as the words come out of my mouth I suddenly remember that there was an assignment due this morning that I totally forgot about. Not the best way to keep my grades up. But I'm not going to let that little mistake get me down. I just got a callback, and Rory might be there. I'm not going to let reality get me down today.

CHAPTER 16

My summer science class is filled with kids from other schools, so I only know a few of them and, of course, Nevin. Some kids are taking the class to replace a not-so-hot grade, like me, but it seems like most of the kids are taking it to get advanced placement next year or because their family moved and they need to finish the requirement.

I walk into class and see that there is a seat next to this girl Allison, who I talked to last week. I walk over to join her at her table, but before I can get to the seat, Nevin stops me. "So how is milady this fine day?" he asks in his strange Middle-earth accent. He's wearing a brown felt hat with oddly shaped patches sewn on it.

"What in the world is on top of your head?" I ask.

"Ah, I see my authentic Middle-earth head cozy has caught your attention."

"Nevin, it's eighty degrees out and it looks like you're wearing a dead cat on your head," I say, and walk away toward the seat next to Allison, but someone has taken it since Nevin delayed me.

Before I can find another place to sit, Mr. Evans comes in and says, "We have a lot to cover today, so if you haven't found a seat, please find one, and let's start with the chapter on 'Hypothesis.'" I look around the room. The only empty seats are at the table in front of me, where Nevin has plopped himself down. I look around the room one last time in a desperate attempt to find an empty chair somewhere other than next to Nevin, but there are no other options. I put my bag on the table and take my seat next to Nevin. He looks up from his notebook and smiles at me. I'm stuck with him and his head cozy for *one* class. How bad can it be?

Mr. Evans is saying something about inquiry. I know I should be taking notes, since Nevin and most of the other kids in class seem to be writing furiously, but I never know exactly what I should be writing down. "Oh, wait," Mr. Evans says, and moves from the front of the room back to his desk. "I forgot to write down your lab partners."

Lab partners is serious business. That is who you

are stuck working with all summer. I try to make eye contact with Allison, who seems like she would make a cool partner, but she is whispering with the curly-haired girl who took my seat next to her. I scan the room and see if there is anyone else who I can make eye contact with. I feel like a sinking submarine tapping out a futile SOS call.

Mr. Evans grabs a pen from his desk and says, "Since you're already sitting in pairs, let's just use these for the summer. Oh, and this will also be the partner you will have during our final exam at the City Science Center and Museum."

I want to stand up on my chair and shout, "Nooo! No! No! No!" Of all the days to get stuck sitting next to Nevin, I do it on the day lab partners are assigned. This is not happening. Mr. Evans starts going table by table, writing down the lab partners in his notebook. Nevin knows better than to even look at me while this is happening, but once Mr. Evans gets to our table and writes down our names, we both realize our fate is sealed. Nevin looks over at me and smiles.

"Looks like we're going to be spending a significant amount of time together during this solstice with the longest of amplitudes."

"Nevin, no offense, and I have no idea what that actually means, but please don't say it again."

"Affirmative, milady."

"Can you just say, 'Sure, Cassie'? You know the way people talk. Please."

"Sure, Cassie," he says very quietly.

I lean back in my chair and look up at the ceiling. I would rather get to know one of the new kids in class, but maybe working with Nevin won't be so bad. I look over at him as he furiously takes notes and realize he is writing with a pen that is in the shape of a hobbit. On the other hand this could be one of those summers that makes me look forward to the start of school.

CHAPTER 17

As soon as class is over, I dash out of the room and almost run out of the building. If I am totally focused, I can make it to my callback on time, maybe even a little early. I jog home and go straight to my bedroom and change. It's important to wear the same thing to a callback that you do to an audition, and luckily, I just threw the lime-green-striped top with the broad scoop neck and the thin periwinkle cardigan with small purple buttons that I wore last week on top of my desk. So they may not be perfectly clean, but at least they're not totally wrinkled. I pull the top on over my head, smooth out any stray wrinkles with the palms of my hands, and grab the folder of head-shots and résumés I keep ready in my desk drawer. It's rare that they need a new headshot or résumé at the callback, but when they do need one and you have it, you seem very professional.

I walk out of the building and don't break my stride until I am in front of Betsy Barnes Casting. I take a deep breath before I open the door. This would be such an amazing spot to book. It's national, so that means my dad could see it at any time. Also, there is a chance that Rory could have a callback too.

It looks like they have called back about two dozen kids. Last time this place was a zoo, but today the energy is calm and serious. I scan the room quickly to see if Rory has also gotten a callback. I don't see him. I sign in and wait in a chair close to the door to the studio. The casting assistant comes out of the studio and calls in the next group, and I sneak a peek into the studio. It looks like there are a ton of people in there. I hate callbacks where everybody and their grandmother is in the rooms. On smaller spots you just get the director and the client and a few random people. I guess this is a major spot, because it looks like there are at least a dozen people at the tables behind the camera.

I turn back in my chair and see Phoebe on the other side of the room, looking a bit frantic. I assumed she would be here, since she is perfect for the girlfriend role. She had a lot of years of not booking anything, so I am totally happy for her.

"Cassie, I'm so glad you're here. Have you seen Liam?" Phoebe asks as she walks over to me.

"Have you seen you-know-who?" I ask, but my voice is almost a whisper.

"No," she says, but I can tell she is really distracted. "Liam isn't answering his cell, and he promised he would meet me before the callback. I'm going to see if he's in the lobby. If they call my name, tell them I'll be right back," she says.

"Is everything all right?"

"Yeah, I guess. I just really need him here."

"No problem. I'll let you know if I see him," I tell her, and she heads down the hall toward the elevators. As soon as she is out of sight, Rory appears from around the corner. I take a deep breath in and then let it out. He is wearing the same royal blue shirt he wore to the audition last week. At first I can't believe he's here, but then I realize that's ridiculous. Casting directors absolutely love Rory as much as all the girls my age on the circuit do. How could Rory not get a callback? He signs in, and he can't help but see me.

"Hi, Monique," he says, his smile all teeth and charm.

What do I do? Do I correct him or do I just

say nothing? "Hey, Rory," I say, trying to find the right way to tell him that my name is actually Cassie. Before I can find the words, the door to the studio opens and Neil, my favorite casting assistant, announces the names of the people in the next group. The last name he says is mine. I stand up as if to go in, but then I don't move. Neil is standing only two feet away from me but still, I don't move. I can't tell if this is a disaster or an opportunity.

Rory looks confused, as if he is going to say, *Your name is Monique, not Cassie! Sit back down.* But then Neil taps me on the shoulder and says, "Cassie, c'mon. Everyone else is already in."

Rory looks at me and realizes that my name must be Cassie. He gives me this embarrassed grin and then sweeps his fist in front of his body and hits himself in the forehead in a funny way. I giggle but don't have a chance to say anything, since I'm the last kid to enter the room. He knows that we kids have to appear super professional at every second of an audition or we get a bad reputation fast.

I have never had an easier time pretending to be happy at a callback in my entire life. Rory not only smiled at me, but we definitely had some type of quality interaction. He was even goofing around for me. During the entire callback my smile is bright, open, and real.

Finally the director says, "Thanks, everyone. I think we have what we need," and we are dismissed. Now we just need to wait to get a call from our agents. I don't want to appear too anxious, so I make sure I'm the last one out of the studio, right behind Neil, who calls more names off his sheet and brings in the next group.

Rory is seated right next to where I was sitting, and when he sees me he gets up and says, "Hi, Cassie. That's your name. *Cassie.*"

"Yeah," I say. "That's me. I'm Cassie."

"I'm, like, so sorry. I was calling you Monique. I'm so sorry," he says.

"That's okay," I say, standing across from him. He's a little taller than I am, so I actually have to raise my eyes a bit to look into his.

"I just thought your name was Monique because, you know, Monique is such a pretty name, and, well, you're so pretty, so I guess I just put the two together. Not that Cassie isn't a pretty name too."

RR just called me pretty. He directly called me pretty. The phrase was, "well, you're so pretty." That's what he just said. I want to jump up and down. I want to tear up my headshot into little pieces of paper and use them as confetti. However, I know this is an important moment where I need to act just a bit cooler than I actually may be.

"Thanks," I say, making sure I have a soft but not too enthusiastic smile on my face.

"No prob," he says. "So is Cassie short for Cassandra?"

Everyone always asks me this, and sometimes I just say yes so I don't have to go into the whole story. Uh, no," I begin. "My full name is actually Cassiopeia."

"You too?" he asks.

"What do you mean?" Is it possible that Rory is named after a constellation too?

"Free-spirit parents. I'm actually named after a lyric in some folk song. Isn't it awful?"

Wow. Rory has hippie parents too. How is this possible? I mean, he looks so clean-cut and sort of preppie at auditions. Then I think of how I look at auditions. I don't look anything like the family I come from. We talk for a little bit about the annoyances of hippie parents and how we both hate granola and anything having to do with sing-a-longs or camping.

"How did your callback go?" he asks.

"They're going pretty quickly. You won't have to wait too long."

"That's good. I have a soccer game tonight, and I want to make sure I have enough time to warm up before the game."

"What position do you play?" I ask. I know that when a boy starts talking about playing sports, you can always ask what position he plays, unless it's something like bowling or golf. Then you're supposed to ask something else, but I can't remember what it is.

"I'm usually a forward, but sometimes I—"

The door to the studio swings open, and the casting assistant announces a list of names, including Rory's.

"Well, I better head in. Maybe I'll see you on set," he says, and walks toward the open studio door.

"Yeah, sure! Totally. Absolutely! That would be, like, awesome!" I say. My previous appearance of cool aloofness crumbles a bit with each phrase. Luckily, he's walking into the studio, so he barely hears my verbal explosion.

Once the studio door closes and Rory and I are in separate rooms, I finally feel like I can breathe again. I walk out of the casting office and take the elevator down to the lobby. As I walk out onto the sidewalk of the busy street, I realize that I am still in a state of shock. Rory and I had an actual conversation, and he actually called me pretty. It still doesn't seem real.

I consider taking a taxi back to the apartment building, so I don't forget a single detail of my interaction with RR before I can tell Ginger, but the streets are so packed with summer traffic that I figure I might as well walk.

CHAPTER 18

I get back and head straight to Ginger's apartment. My knuckles sound like a machine gun on the hard metal door. The door opens and Ginger appears. "There you are." She doesn't need to say another word. The familiar and comforting smell of frying buttered bread and melted cheese reminds me of my mistake.

"Ginger, I totally forgot we were planning to make grilled cheeses," I say, following her into the kitchen.

"I tried your cell phone a few times but no answer. I was beginning to get worried."

I grab my cell out of my bag, and sure enough, I see the list of missed calls from Ginger. "I had to turn it off for my callback, and with all the excitement I forgot to turn it back on."

"Callback? Well, that explains it." Ginger goes

over to the kitchen. "You're lucky I saved you half of my sandwich." She puts a plate with a slightly cold but still delicious–looking half grilled cheese on it in front of me and then pulls a bag of chips from the top of the fridge and pours a generous serving onto the plate. "I can warm it up for you if you want."

"No, this is fine," I say. "Thanks." I try to sound as friendly as possible, since I can tell by her tone she is a little mad at me for blowing off our lunch plan. She has every right to be a little mad. I should have texted her to let her know I was going to be late. It was wrong of me, and I feel bad for being a not–so–great friend. "Ginger, I'm really sorry."

"That's okay. You'll make it up to me, since YOU are doing the dishes." She announces this last part with a flourish, so I know immediately what it means.

"You didn't!"

"I did."

"In English or Chinese?" I ask.

"In English, mostly. My Chinese vocabulary is primarily focused on the weather and how to bargain for a chicken in the market."

"Oh, Ginger. This is amazing news. I want to

hear everything." I take a bite out of my grilled cheese and listen with rapt attention.

"There's not much to tell. I basically went up to him and said, 'Hi, I'm Ginger.' And he said he knew that, because he's been waiting for me to talk to him since last year."

"That's amazing."

"I know. Anyway, it turns out we were both adopted, but he was born in the US. Still, we talked a lot about that. And that's all."

"Stop." I tell her, and just like the casting director in an audition, I give her some constructive criticism. "I want you to tell me the story again, only this time, don't leave anything out. I need detail. I want to be able to see the scene in my mind."

Ginger tells me the story again, and this time she includes all the relevant details, like bits of dialogue and a description of what everything looked like and where they were. As she tells the story, I go over to the sink and start doing the dishes, since a deal is a deal.

I finish drying the last dish and sit down at the kitchen table next to Ginger. "So I didn't tell you *who* was at my callback yet."

"Phoebe?" she asks.

"No," I say, and look down. I always feel sort of weird when Ginger mentions Phoebe. I've told Ginger everything about Phoebe, and Ginger has seen Phoebe on TV hundreds of times. Who hasn't? But I never really talk to Phoebe about Ginger. It just doesn't come up. A couple of times Ginger has suggested we invite Phoebe out to the movies with us or something like that. I always make up some excuse as to why I can't invite Phoebe, but the truth is, I like keeping my two worlds apart. Sure Ginger knows every detail about both worlds, but that's different from actually having those worlds collide.

"Who was it?" Ginger asks, and then suddenly she figures it out on her own. "Rory!"

"YES!" I say.

Her eyes widen. "Cassie Herold, I can't believe you let me go on and on about Ming-wei when this whole time you actually have news. "Tell me everything," she says. "Do not leave out a single detail. Do you understand, Cassie? I want to hear everything!"

"Hey, I think we have some of those organic juice Popsicles in the freezer at my house. Let's go get them and take a walk so I can tell you the whole story."

Is there anything better than sharing a Popsicle with your best friend on a hot summer afternoon and telling her the story of how the cute boy you've liked for months has just called you pretty?

CHAPTER 19

"*Absolutely not, Michael! No! You cannot do it* this way!"

As I walk into our apartment later, I can hear my mother shouting at my father on the phone. I don't know why they have to argue so much whenever they talk. Can't they just get along better, like they did when I was a kid or even before I was born? My mom used to tell the story of how they went to a Nirvana concert together in grad school when they lived in Seattle and how they walked home in the rain. I love that story and wish they would try taking a walk in the rain again.

My mother is in her bedroom with the door closed, but I can still hear every word of her side of the conversation through our potato-chip-thin apartment walls. I sit on the floor outside her door and just listen.

"Michael. This needs to come from you and in person!" my mom shouts. Are they talking about money? They used to fight about money all the time. My dad would want to treat us to something special, and my mom would tell him we couldn't afford it, and then back and forth until someone just stormed out of the room.

"I will not do it. Do you hear me? I won't." Her voice is calmer now, but she is still upset. "You can't just tell her something like this over the phone."

Now this phrase gets my attention. The "her" she is talking about must be me. I don't think I actually want to know what they're talking about. Before I can hear another word, I knock on my mom's door and burst into her room.

"Hi, Mom," I say in my best and brightest commercial voice. I might not be able to get them to see eye to eye on whatever they are fighting about, but maybe I can at least interrupt them. "Who are you talking to?" I ask as innocently as possible.

I am like a human Band-Aid in my parents' fights. They must have read some handbook somewhere that said not to fight in front of your child. Whenever they are fighting and I walk into a room, they immediately stop. I don't know why they don't realize that a person doesn't need to be in the actual room where someone is screaming in order to hear them.

"Oh, Cassie. I didn't hear you come in." My mom has obviously been crying. Her face is wet and red, and she tries to discreetly wipe her eyes dry, but I can tell something bad is going on.

"Is everything okay?" I ask, not sure if I want the answer.

"Of course, dear," she says, her voice cracking. "I'm just having a conversation with your father." She gets up out of the chair she is sitting in and grabs her purse. She takes out her wallet and hands me a twenty-dollar bill. "Would you run down to Good Foods and buy some soy milk and get some sorbet or something for yourself while you're there?"

I'm being bought off. I know it and she knows I know it. I could say something or ask to talk to my dad, but the mood in the bedroom is so intense that I just nod, take the money from my mother, and head to the store. If the "her" they were talking about is me, then I guess I'll find out soon enough.

CHAPTER 20

Waiting for the phone to ring makes everything go more slowly. I don't have any go-sees scheduled for today, there is no summer school, and Ginger is at Chinese school. My life is in a state of suspended animation. I both don't want my phone to ring *and* I want it to ring. On one hand it could be my dad, calling me to tell me whatever horrible thing my mom wants him to tell me. On the other it could be Honey, calling me to tell me I booked the Seven Sails spot. I put my cell phone down on the kitchen table with the screen facing up, so I will know right away who is calling. If it's my dad, I'll just let it go to voice mail.

Since there is homework due tomorrow in class, I figure I had better start working on it now. The only way I can even consider doing homework over the summer is to make sure I am totally set up before beginning any type of work. I put a generous serving of my favorite nacho-flavored potato chips into a bowl and pour myself a large glass of fruit punch topped off with a splash of lemon soda. Then I grab the bag of carob-covered raisins my mom bought at Good Foods the other day and put them on the tray with the other treats. I put the tray on the table next to my notebook and other school stuff and then take a seat at the table.

I'm supposed to write two pages about a scientific topic I would like to research and then a page about why I would like to research it. I turn to a fresh page in my notebook and just stare at the blank lines. I look over at my cell phone in case I missed a call or text. Then I stare back at the blank page. How am I supposed to write about a topic I would like to research when there is nothing I would like to research? Worse than that, I have to write about *why* I would like to research something that I really don't want to research.

I stare at the blank page, hoping something will happen to inspire me.

Nothing happens except the ice in my drink melts, so I get up from the table to go to the freezer to get a few fresh cubes. I take the ice tray out, and as soon as I hold it over the sink, I hear my phone ring.

Please be Honey. Please be Honey. I dump the ice tray in the sink and leap toward the table to grab my phone. I look at the screen before answering. YES!

"Hi, Honey," I say, unable to hide my excitement.

"Hi, Cas. I don't have any news on the Seven Sails spot yet," she says right away. I guess she knows I'm anxious about booking that spot. Who wouldn't want to spend the day in an amusement park? Still, I try to pretend like I'm not even worried about the booking.

"Oh, Seven Sails? Is that the amusement park? Oh, yeah. Now I remember."

"Doll, I want to know if I can clear you for some dates for a major campaign that's coming up. It's for Happy Family Cruises."

"Awesome!" I say. "We went on when of those cruises to the Cayman Islands a few years ago. It was amazing," I tell Honey and then look over to the bookshelf where we keep all the framed family photos. These pictures remind me of what it's like to be part of a happy family. There's one of me as a baby coming home from the hospital, a picture of my parents on their wedding day, and a wicker frame with a picture of me and my family during the cruise a few years ago. We are standing under a canopy of bright magenta hibiscus; our faces are lightly sunburnt and our smiles natural and relaxed. My parents are even holding hands. I love this picture not only because we look so happy, but also because at that moment we *were* so happy. I almost tell Honey they should just use this picture for the commercial.

"Well, let me give you these dates to see if you can take the appointment," Honey says.

"Sure," I say, and grab my appointment book. She tells me the audition and hold dates for the booking, and they are smack-dab in the middle of my summer school class. The shoot date is even the same exact date as our final exam at the Science Center.

"Sorry, Honey. I can't do those dates," I tell her.

"Too bad," she says. "It was a pretty big campaign for Happy Family Cruises. They're launching a new website, and this campaign will—" She stops speaking midsentence and then says, "Hold on, Cassie. This might be the call we've both been waiting for."

My heart starts pounding. Could this be news

about the Seven Sails spot? I sit down at the kitchen table and take a deep breath, trying to calm myself, but my foot keeps tapping uncontrollably.

"Cassie!" Honey shouts from the other end of the phone. "I have some good news. You booked the spot for the amusement park."

"YES!" I shout, matching her enthusiasm.

"Oh, this is going to be a fun one," Honey says.

"Do you happen to have the full booking list?" I ask as casually as possible. I would hate for Honey to figure out how much I like Rory. I don't want her to think I'm unprofessional.

"Sure," she says. "There are six kids playing the friends. You . . ." She reads the names, and the third one is Phoebe Marks, so I know I will have at least one friend on set. Then Honey reads the last name, ". . . and Rory Roberts."

"Sounds good," I say, underplaying how excited I actually am. Honey tells me she'll e-mail me all the details for the shoot and the wardrobe fitting and I hang up.

I am actually going to be on set all day with RR, who just happens to have told me that he thinks I'm pretty.

CHAPTER 21

After I got the phone call about my booking, I told myself I would spend that evening working on my science homework. After I talked to Phoebe on the phone for a few hours about the booking, I told myself that I would get up extra early and do my assignment before class. After I overslept, I told myself I would think of a really good excuse on my way to class.

As soon as I get to class, Mr. Evans says, "Everyone take out the assignment that's due today. I want you to work with your lab partner to further define your topic. Each person needs to read their homework out loud to their partner, and I am handing out response sheets that you should use to guide your conversation." I begin to go through some of the random papers in my backpack so I don't stick out. Most of the papers in my backpack are sides from auditions. I also have a few headshots in case I have a last-minute go-see. The class settles into their groups and Nevin taps me on the shoulder.

"I brought in three copies just in case you thought we needed an extra copy for something," Nevin says, handing me his papers. I look down at them and see that he has gone way over the expected word count. "Do you want to go first or do you want me to start?"

"Ah . . ." I hesitate. "Why don't you go first?" I say. Maybe I can use Nevin's overachieverness to my advantage. "And read slowly. Very, *very* slowly. I want to make sure I hear every word."

Nevin looks at me with a bit of confusion on his face. "You do?"

"Of course," I say. "I'm very interested in . . ." I grab the papers with his assignment and read the title off the first page. "'The Role Real Science Plays in Science Fiction.'" Is he serious? Does Nevin want to be a dork for the rest of his life? Why not just come to class wearing a T-shirt that says, I AM THE BIGGEST NERD IN THE UNIVERSE? Then I look down and see that he's wearing a T-shirt with a picture of Albert Einstein on it, and I realize he already is. I can't believe I have to spend the summer listening to Nevin talk about hobbits and spaceships and whatever other boring dork stuff he wants to write about.

"Really? You're interested in science fiction?"

I kind of do a head-shake-closed-mouth-smile thing that could be interpreted as anything from "Where's the bathroom?" to "This sausage is spicy!" Of course, Nevin takes this as a yes.

"Great, because I've already started doing the research, and it is absolutely fascinating."

"Well, whatever you do, read *slowly*, okay?"

"Sure," he says, and then begins reading the first sentence of his assignment with the speed of a taxi at rush hour. Perfect. At this rate he won't be finished until next Thursday, or at least until the end of class. I immediately tune out and look at my watch. If I can just keep him talking, I can avoid having to tell Mr. Evans that I did not do my assignment. I'll just bring it to the next class and he'll never know the difference.

Nevin is saying something about photons or phasers, but my mind is miles away. I'm thinking about the wardrobe fitting I have scheduled later in the day and the shoot this weekend with Rory.

CHAPTER 22

Getting up early for school is almost impossible.
Getting up early for a booking is easy. We need to
be at the transport van at six a.m. My mom insists
on seeing me to the van, although I have been able
to convince her not to come to the shoot with me.
Some of the kids my age still travel to sets with their
parents, but a lot of kids have started going on their
own. There is always someone on set in charge of
minors, so the truth is, our parents just sit there.
Some of the parents get really into being on set, but
my mom always hated being shuffled from area to
area and having to wait for endless retakes. I imagine
that if you're not on camera, the whole thing can be
rather boring.

Usually I would just roll out of bed for a booking,
since I know there will be someone on location to
do my hair and makeup and put me in some cute

outfit. But today I make sure I look presentable, because there is a chance I will see Rory in the van.

We take a cab to the corner where the van is picking everyone up. Since it's so early in the morning, we fly up streets that are usually bumper-to-bumper. The sun is just beginning to rise, and the shadows are giving way to the glow of a new day. During the ride my mom lectures me on how she only lets me do commercials because she believes they are good real-life experience. I almost laugh when she says this. There is absolutely nothing real-life about them. Real life is messy and boring and filled with homework and curfews and disappointments. Commercials are picture perfect. Everything looks shiny and new, and there's never a hair out of place. Still, I listen to my mom and nod. The last thing I want to do is get into an argument with her in a cab on the way to a booking.

There are three vans on the street corner and a bunch of kids and adults standing around them. I see a woman with a clipboard, who I assume is the person in charge of minors. My mom signs me in for the shoot, gives me a few final reminders, and then gets back in the cab to go home and back to sleep, I imagine.

"If you have checked in with me, please go to the first van, which will leave in two minutes!" shouts the woman with the clipboard. I walk over to the van, hoping I will see Rory signing in, but nothing. I climb into the van and see an Asian girl with short bangs. I can tell this is one of her first bookings, since it looks like she got up early just to curl her hair. You never "do" anything to yourself the day of a booking, because whatever you "do," the stylists will want to "do" differently.

"Hi, I'm Cassie," I say, walking toward the back of the van.

"I'm Jasmine," the girl says, smiling. "Can I ask you a question?"

"Shoot," I say, plopping down my bag and sitting next to her.

"This is my first commercial. Do these shoots always start so early? The sun's barely up." She tries to stifle a yawn as she talks.

"Not always," I say, "but usually. The boys are *so* lucky. They sometimes get a later call, since they don't have to spend so much time in hair and makeup."

"On the other hand," Jasmine says, "they also don't get to have someone do their hair and their makeup!"

We both giggle, and I can tell we're going to be friends.

"We're just waiting for one more girl," some adult with a walkie-talkie barks into the van. I know Phoebe booked the lead role in this spot and her call time was even earlier, so I guess this will be the girl playing the third friend.

Finally the last person arrives. Everyone knows, or at least has seen, Brittany Rush. She has probably appeared in more commercials than any other person on the planet. When she gets on the van, she barely says hello. She just sits down, closes her eyes, and takes a nap. Since it's so early, everyone else in the van, adults included, uses the time to catch up on some sleep.

CHAPTER 23

I'm still only half-awake when the van pulls into the amusement park. There are a few hours until it opens to the public, so the parking lot is empty except for the vans and trailers with all the wardrobe and equipment. Once we stop, the van door slides open and a woman in jeans and a T-shirt tells us her name is Shirley and that she is in charge of minors. She gives us our instructions for the morning, but before we head off to sign in, I hear her say, "The van with the boys should be here soon." That means Rory will be here soon. I decide I had better sign in and head straight to wardrobe and makeup, since I want to look my best when Rory arrives.

I love walking around the set in the morning before production has begun. It always has this feeling of orchestrated chaos. To get to the makeup trailer I have to walk through the entrance to the amusement park, where an army of set designers is making the perfectly manicured lawn look even more perfect. At first it looks like they're just adding to the rows and rows of flowers with additional ones, but as I get closer I see that they are actually sticking fake flowers in among the real ones. I've seen this dozens of times. Of course, in person it looks weird, but through the lens of the camera those fake flowers will look realer than the real ones. I smile to myself and admire their vibrant color. Who's to say those fake flowers are any less real than the ones grown from seed?

I sign in and check my wardrobe as fast as I can so I can make it to the makeup trailer to see Phoebe. I open the door, and the bright fluorescent lights sting my eyes. I see that they are putting the finishing touches on her. Her eyes are closed and a skinny guy in skinnier jeans is lightly brushing something on her eyelids while a not-so-skinny woman with tattoos on her shoulders is arranging Phoebe's hair so the curls are just perfect. The counter in front of where Phoebe is sitting is a parade of the latest and greatest cosmetics and hair products. The stylists on a shoot always have inside information about what new trends are developing, so I always try to pay attention to what they use. On the counter in front of Phoebe are rows of tackle boxes that are usually used to carry bait to a fishing hole. In this alternate universe all the stylists use them to organize their products. I love peeking into them and seeing all the blushes, lip liners, and powders arranged neatly by hue.

"Okay, Phoebe. You're done," the guy stylist says, and she pops out of the chair, comes over to me, and gives me one of her tight hugs while keeping her face turned up to the ceiling so her makeup doesn't smudge.

"Is he here yet?" she asks as discreetly as possible.

"No," I tell her. The adults in the room are going over the script for the day, so we have a few minutes to gossip.

"Well, I heard them say that they're shooting the girls in the morning and that we might not see any of the boys until the afternoon. Did you see my friend Brittany?"

"I didn't know you were friends with her." The truth is, Brittany seemed kind of stuck-up in the van. She barely said a word to Jasmine or me, but maybe she was just tired. If she's friends with Phoebe, she can't be all bad.

The loudspeaker in the makeup trailer crackles and announces, "I need leads on set. Phoebe and Doug to their first mark."

"I better go," Phoebe says. "See you out there." She heads out of the makeup trailer, and I take her spot in the makeup chair.

I'm grateful that the boys won't be on set just yet because it means Rory will get to see me as Commercial Cassie, not boring Everyday Cassie. I look straight ahead at myself in the mirror and smile. I'm ready to be transformed.

CHAPTER 24

I spend the morning in commercial bliss, running around the amusement park, riding rides and hanging out. It's the way any other girl might spend a warm summer day with her friends. The only difference is that entire rides are shut down for us just so we can ride them over and over, lights and cameras follow our every move, and a professional stylist is only a few yards away in case even a single hair is out of place. It's a great day, but it's also a lot of work. When it comes time for lunch, I'm exhausted from having so much fun.

We are given a ninety-minute break for lunch, so the girls and I go back to our dressing rooms to change into our regular clothes. Eating while in wardrobe is not allowed. I knock on Phoebe's dressing room door so we can finish getting ready together. As I comb my hair, Phoebe straps on her sandals.

"Are you ready?" she asks.

Suddenly I feel nervous for the first time today. You would think shooting a national commercial for an amusement park would make me nervous. This spot will be seen by tens of thousands of people, maybe even my dad, but being in front of the camera has never made me nervous. However, the thought of walking into the catering tent and sitting next to Rory has me totally rattled.

As we walk out of our trailer, I ask Phoebe, "What do you think I should say to him?"

"Uh, how about 'hello'?" she says with complete sincerity.

"I mean after that!"

Phoebe thinks for a second and then looks at me and says, "I have absolutely no idea. Most of the conversations I've had with boys in that way have been at go-sees, reading off cue cards, or at a booking where a director is telling me exactly what to do."

It's true. We go-see girls have much more real-life experience from the parts of our lives that have nothing to do with real life. If only there were a way to make real life more like our commercial lives.

When we get to the catering tent, we spot the

table of kids. Jasmine is there with Rory and the other three boys who have booked the spot. One is a kid I have known for years, Doug, who's playing Phoebe's boyfriend, and the other kids are new. Brittany said she was going to skip lunch and rest in her dressing room.

We walk through the food line. I'm so nervous I barely grab anything to eat. I just put some apple wedges and a few carrot sticks on a plate and grab a diet soda and a chocolate cupcake. Not exactly a balanced meal, but the cupcake looked too good to pass up. As we leave the line, the table of kids spots us and Jasmine waves to us to join her. "Here we go," Phoebe whispers in my ear. I take a deep breath, smile, and walk over to the table.

"Do you guys all know each other?" Jasmine asks the group as we take our seats. I am sitting directly across from Rory, which is nerve-racking because I'm worried our knees are going to bump or something.

"Yeah," Rory says. "I know Phoebe and *Monique*." When he says the name Monique, his lips reveal a playful smile, and he almost winks at me. He is so amazingly cute that I just want to study his face and take a picture of it in my mind.

The other kids who know me are a little confused

when they hear Rory call me Monique. A look of terror flashes across Phoebe's face, and being a good friend, she jumps in. "Uh, actually her name is—"

Rory cuts her off. "I know, I know. It's Cassie. Monique is just a little inside joke that we share. How you doing, Cas?"

Phoebe looks at me, her eyes as wide as Ping-Pong balls. I'm sure the mention of an "inside joke" between Rory and me has given her a shock. I'll have to explain everything when we're back in our dressing rooms.

"The morning was fun, Rory. We got to ride the Storm Twister over and over," I tell him.

Stephen, the kid sitting next to Rory, lets out a loud groan. "Uhhhh!"

Rory turns to him and says, "Look, bro, I told you it's all gonna be fine." He looks down at the full plate in front of Stephen and says, "But maybe you should lay off the chili dogs until after we wrap."

"What's wrong?" Jasmine asks as Stephen pushes his plate of food away from him.

"Well . . . ah . . . Stephen gets a little sick when he goes around in circles. He told me during the van ride here."

Suddenly I remember something my mom taught

me that she learned from one of her hippy-dippy healers. "If you feel sick, you should just press here and here with your fingers." I put my index fingers on his forehead over the pressure points my mom showed me for dealing with nausea.

"That's so cool," Rory says. Stephen immediately begins to practice putting his fingers on the pressure points. I don't know whether it will actually work, but at least giving him something to do will take his mind off the spinning.

Everyone starts trying out the pressure points, but Rory looks directly into my eyes and says, "That was really nice of you, Cassie."

I smile at him, but I'm too overwhelmed by his directness to really look straight at him. Instead I let my eyes half focus on my plate of carrots and apple wedges. When I finally look up, I see Phoebe chugging her can of root beer. She finishes the last drop and says, "Boy, this shoot has made me thirsty. Rory, would you be an angel and get me another soda from the catering truck?"

Of course there is no reason why Phoebe can't get a can of soda herself, and Rory sees through her little trick. "Sure, Phoebe. Wanna come with me, Monique?"

Phoebe gives me a look that seems to say, *GET! UP! NOW!* so I say, "Sure. Why not?" and remind myself to thank Phoebe for being an amazing friend.

Rory and I walk over to where all the tables are set up near the catering truck. I have no idea what to say. None. I'm just so excited that I know I should say something. Luckily, he takes care of that.

"I had to miss a soccer practice for the shoot today," he says, and then I remember that he plays soccer.

"Oh, that's too bad," I say.

"No, it's awesome," he says. "The sun is brutal today. I'd much rather be here."

Whoops. Miscalled that one. I quickly try to back it up. "Yeah. That's awesome. I just mean it's too bad . . . uh . . . about . . . uh . . . the sun. You know." What *am* I saying? Even I don't know what I'm saying. Seriously, I have absolutely no idea what I'm saying, and I'm the one saying it. There is no way that can be good.

Then Rory says, "You mean the like frozen layer?"

Now I have no idea what he is talking about, but still I agree. "Yeah," I say, and nod my head.

He nods his head too and says, "Yeah, I heard

there's a hole in it, which is why I gotta wear so much of that sunscreen goop during practice. I hate it."

Then it suddenly dawns on me that he means the ozone layer and not the frozen layer. So he's not the brightest bulb in the tanning bed. He's still the cutest. I decide not to correct him on the ozone thing and instead listen to him tell me a play-by-play of his latest soccer game as we grab a few sodas and head back to the table with the other kids.

I walk as slowly as I can on the way back. I don't want our time alone together to end. I want us to walk like this side by side all the way back to the city.

When we get to the table, we pass out the extra sodas we got for everybody before we're interrupted by an anxious production assistant.

"I need you boys on set for some lighting tests," the PA says, pointing at the boys and shouting from across the room. Part of me is upset that this moment is being interrupted, but another part of me is glad I don't have to think of anything else to say.

The boys get up from the table, and I say to Rory, "See you on set."

"Totally," he says. The boys head out, but Rory lingers just a bit and says to me, "We should hang out sometime." Before I can say anything in response, he breaks into a jog and catches up with the other boys and heads out of the tent.

The three of us girls don't say anything until the last boy is safely out of earshot, and then Phoebe begins. "Excuse me, but *O* period. *M* period."

"Let me finish this," Jasmine says. "G freaking period. Rory totally likes you."

"You think?" I say. Sure he was being awfully sweet to me during the break, but he's sort of like that with everyone.

"*Think?*" Phoebe says. "I don't think. I know. He was totally flirting with you the whole time. You even have an inside joke. When did that happen?"

"And what did he whisper to you just before he left?" Jasmine asks.

"Uh . . . uh . . ." I'm not sure what to say. I want to tell them everything, but there's also a part of me that wants to keep some of this private. Luckily, we're interrupted again before I have to actually say anything. The same PA who called the boys back on set is standing at our table.

"Girls, they want to make some wardrobe adjustments for the afternoon, so you need to head over to the wardrobe trailer before we get you back on set."

We gather up our things and head out of the tent, but as we're getting ready, Phoebe says, "I'm willing to bet that you and Rory are totally dating by the end of summer."

"I agree with Phoebe. The way he was talking to you and the way he was looking at you. Totally," Jasmine says, nodding.

I follow Jasmine and Phoebe out of the tent. Of course I would like to be dating Rory by the end of the summer, but what am I supposed to do next? Life is much easier when you have a storyboard in front of you that tells you exactly what you're supposed to say and shows you exactly what you're supposed to do.

CHAPTER 25

After the shoot I'm exhausted but in this satisfying way. Not only did I just finish a national campaign, but I also spent most of the day with the boy in the number one spot on my Crush List. The van drops me off in front of my apartment building, and all I want to do is go upstairs, take a cool shower, watch some mindless DVD, and go to sleep.

As I stand at the front door searching for my key, I hear a voice coming from inside the apartment. It's not my mother's voice, but it's too muffled to make out who it might be exactly. Classes are over at the university, so it can't be a student. I assume it must be some other professor from the math department. I finally find my key and open the door.

"Dad!" I shout when I see my father sitting on the couch with my mom. I run over and hug him.

"I didn't know you were going to be here. This is so great!"

"How was your shoot?" my mom asks.

"Exhausting," I say, throwing my bag on the table. "But also really good." I can't believe we are all in the same room together. It's been months and months since anything like this has even come close to happening. This must mean something important, something really important. Then it dawns on me. Maybe they are finally finished with the "trial separation" and are ready to try being a real family again.

This is the perfect ending to a perfect day.

The fact that they're in the same room is a good sign. Whenever my dad has been in town before, I usually went downstairs to meet him, or he came and got me when he knew my mom would not be around. The fact that they are sitting on the couch without strangling each other has got to be a good sign.

"Hey, we should all go down to that pizzeria on Mercer Street and get Italian ices like we used to do. You know, to celebrate."

"What do you mean?" my dad asks.

"To celebrate the fact that Dad has stopped traveling. You know, we can celebrate being a family again." If I can just get us all out together at the same place, at the same time, maybe they'll see that things can be better. They just *have* to.

My mom looks at my dad. Her lips tighten. My dad catches her eye for a second, and then he looks down at the ground. It's pretty clear neither of them feels like celebrating.

"Michael!" my mom says, prodding my dad, but he doesn't say anything. He just keeps looking at the floor.

The silence feels like a weight pressing down on my head. I need to do something, anything.

"You know what?" I say. "I think we have some frozen Soyjoy in the freezer. I'll scoop it out and we can all just stay here and play Monopoly, or we can set up the Wii." I walk over to the kitchen without looking at either of my parents. I go directly to the cupboard above the sink and take out three bowls, but before I can get to the freezer, my father stops me.

"Cassie, stop. Please. We need to talk." His voice is soft and very serious. I study his face for a second. I could just go to the freezer and keep going like everything is okay, but the more I look at my dad's face, the more I see that it looks like he might have been crying earlier. I look at my mom for a second, and her face has the same worried and sad expression.

Cut!

All day long, whenever anything was not right, whenever anything was not perfect, the director would step in and yell, "Cut!" If too much sweat appeared above Stephen's lip or if Phoebe stepped out of the light line or if Jasmine needed to have a brighter, bigger smile, the director would yell, "Cut!" and everything would stop. We'd go back to our original positions and start the scene over again. Where is he now? Where is he when I need someone to stop what is happening, make it better and start from the beginning?

"We need to talk," my dad says again. He goes back to the couch and waves his hand for me to come and join both of them. My mom sits on the other side of the couch, and I reluctantly walk out of the kitchen and take the empty spot between them.

I am silent, waiting for one of them to tell me what I've already figured out, but inside my head I'm yelling at the top of my lungs.

Cut.

Cut!

CUT!

CHAPTER 26

"*Hi, Mr. and Mrs. Ellet,*" *I say after knocking* quietly on the door. Ginger's parents both look at me with sad smiles. Her dad is standing by the door, and her mom is in the kitchen.

"Your parents called and told us you were coming to spend the night," Mr. Ellet says, and hugs me. I try not to cry as he puts his arms around me. "I'm so sorry. Let us know what we can do to help." His beard scratches my face gently.

"Well, I'm making you girls some fresh limeade," Mrs. Ellet says from the kitchen. She wipes her hands on a dish towel and then wheels out of the kitchen to give me a hug. I bend across her wheelchair and hug her back.

Ginger is so lucky. I have never once heard her parents yell at each other, and they only argue over silly stuff, like what color to paint the bathroom or who should win an Oscar. Her family might not look like a lot of other families, but Ginger can feel safe knowing they will always stay together.

"Ginger is just making up the trundle bed in her room," Mrs. Ellet says. "If you need any towels or clean sheets, just let me know."

"Thank you," I say quietly. My voice feels dry and scratchy after so much crying.

"I'm going to put a tray of drinks and snacks outside Ginger's door in a minute, so just get it when you're ready. I don't want to disturb you. I know you girls need to talk."

"Thanks," I say without looking either of them in the eye, and head down the hall toward Ginger's room. I'm so glad they let me come over tonight. I just couldn't stay at home. Not tonight. Even my parents, who agree on absolutely nothing, agreed that it would be better if I spent the night here at Ginger's.

I slowly open the door to Ginger's room, and she is in the middle of putting a pillowcase on one of her extra pillows. She stops when she sees me. "Oh, Cassie. I'm so sorry," she says.

I shut the door behind me, and before I can even say a word the tears start again. I can't control them. I hate this feeling of not being in control of my emotions. I think back to earlier in the day when my emotions, or at least what appeared to be my emotions, were part of an orchestrated plan. I hate that my tears appear without any warning and that I have no idea what happens next. I collapse on Ginger's bed, and she sits down next to me and puts her arm around me.

"Do you want to talk about it?" Ginger asks in a way that lets me know I don't have to if I don't want to. But I do want to talk about it. I just don't know what to say.

"I'm just so confused. I mean, I knew they were having problems, but it was supposed to be a *trial* separation. I knew that my dad traveling all the time wasn't helping the situation, but I still thought it was all going to work out. I just thought they needed a break from each other or something like that, but . . . a divorce?"

"A divorce is pretty serious," Ginger says.

"That's not even the worst part. My dad is going to take a job in California. California, Ginger. Like, on the other side of the country. I'll never see him."

"Why? What did he say?"

I try to think back to just a short while ago. The

whole thing is such a blur. I remember going to sit on the couch, and after that I can only remember bits and pieces. It was like an out-of-body experience.

"My dad said something about always loving me but that he just couldn't see himself living with my mom in the apartment and blah, blah, blah." I put my face in a pillow, hoping to stop another flood of tears.

"What's that supposed to mean?"

"I have no idea," I say, my words muffled through the pillow.

How could this day start out so wonderful and end so terribly? I start crying again, and this time I don't try to stop the tears. They just flow and flow and somehow Ginger manages to help me get into the trundle bed. I pull the sheet over me, grateful that I am so exhausted I can just put this day behind me and fall asleep.

CHAPTER 27

That night at Ginger's I have the most amazing dream. I'm in the apartment, only it looks totally different. Where we usually have piles of books or craft projects, there are smooth, clean surfaces. The kitchen is spotless, and all the old, worn furniture has been replaced by bright, shiny, new pieces. It takes me a second to figure out where I am, and even though everything looks different, I am definitely in our apartment.

Then my mom comes in, but instead of her long gray-and-brown braid, her hair is cut short just above her shoulders, and all the gray is totally gone. She's wearing khaki capri pants and a soft green tailored shirt unlike anything she has ever worn before. For once she does not look like a mathematics professor.

She walks over to me and says, "I'm so glad we all booked this spot together."

Of course I'm confused. "What spot?" I ask.

Then my dad enters, wearing a pilot's uniform. "The spot we had the callback for last week." He takes off his pilot's hat and says, "I guess I won't be needing this anymore."

"Oh, Michael," my mom says with a giggle, like a housewife from some seventies sitcom.

Then it suddenly dawns on me. We're in a commercial, the three of us. The apartment is immaculate and my parents look gorgeous. They are smiling at each other and even laughing. No one is yelling about money or work commitments or anything.

A middle-aged guy with a baseball cap runs into the apartment screaming, "Cut! Cut!" The baseball cap and attitude make me think this guy must be the director. He walks over to me and says, "You. You are *ruining* this shoot. You can't wear that, and you don't know your lines or any of the blocking."

I look down at myself and I'm wearing my oldest pair of pajamas—the ones that have a few holes in them. "I'm so, so sorry," I say. "I'll go to wardrobe. I'll change."

"No, no, no," he says. I can tell he's getting angry. "There's no time. We're just going to have to go with what we've got." He flips through pages of a clipboard, and dozens of storyboards from go-sees I've been on over the past few years fly off his clipboard and around the room. I try to grab a few of them to help him, but they blow around so fast I can't seem to get my hand on any of them.

The director speaks through a megaphone like the one used in the Seven Sails shoot. "Mom, I need you over here, and Dad, I need you over here. Daughter, just stay with me and watch what I do, okay?"

My parents start moving into position as lights and cameras and production assistants arrive out of nowhere. I stand behind the director, watching in awe as my parents take their places. I want to run up to them and give them a few pointers before the camera starts rolling. "Don't look into the lens! Don't scrunch your eyes! Smile when you talk!" I try to shout, but nothing comes out.

It doesn't matter because the director yells, "Action!" and my parents talk and move like any of the hundreds of fake moms and fake dads I have auditioned with over the years.

"Perfect!" the director yells. "Perfect!" He turns to me, and even though I am right next to him he uses the megaphone to ask, "Hey, Cassie, how did you get two parents who are so perfect?"

I look at my parents, who seem both familiar and distant at the same time. They smile at me, but their smiles aren't their usual smiles. It's like they're auditioning to play the part of themselves in my picture-perfect idea of our family.

CHAPTER 28

I creep back home the next day when I'm sure no one will be there. I open the door and, after checking that neither of my parents is around, walk directly to the beat-up air-conditioner that sits awkwardly in the windowsill. I turn it on and wait for the warm air to turn colder as I lean over the noisy machine, holding up my hair away from my neck. The air finally changes from wet and warm to cool and dry. I just stand in front of the AC and look around the apartment.

The apartment is small, but all the books and papers make it feel even smaller. A few months ago I booked a spot for Shaw's grocery store, and I remember how clean and perfect the family room in that spot felt. I didn't have any lines. I just followed my fake mom into the kitchen as she talked to my fake dad about how much money she saved. I did a lot of nodding and smiling. The set was on a soundstage in Astoria, and it was pouring rain, but inside fake sunlight streamed through the large windows of the kitchen set. It was so realistic that when I stepped back outside I remember being so confused. How could everything be so camera-ready on the inside and so miserable on the outside?

Our apartment looks like our family. It's messy and overgrown and confusing. I look at the bookshelf next to the hallway and something is different, but at first I can't tell what. I walk over to the bookshelf and stare at it for a few seconds, and then it dawns on me—all three of them are gone. Where are they? I quickly scan all the other shelves in the room. I even look in my parents' bedroom and then my room. They didn't move them, they actually took them down. I can't believe it.

I stare at the only shelf in the entire apartment that is not overflowing with clutter and craft projects, and the emptiness makes me want to cry. Since I can remember there have always been three pictures up on that shelf. I was just looking at them the other day.

One picture is of my parents on their wedding day. It is my favorite picture of them. My mom is young and much thinner. Her hair does not have a drop of gray, and instead of being in her usual thick braid, it's curly and bouncy. My dad is young and handsome, even though he has a silly long beard. They look so much in love that I can ignore the fact that they're getting married in an old barn somewhere upstate and that my mom is wearing a muslin dress she made and embroidered herself, and my dad is wearing, gulp, sandals.

The second framed picture shows me as a baby with both of my parents holding me the day after I was born. I'm wrapped in a yellow blanket, my dad's beard is gone, and my mom has just begun wearing her hair in a braid.

The final picture is from our cruise in the Cayman Islands. All three of us are standing under a canopy of hibiscus, and our happy smiles glow from our freshly sunburnt faces. Where are they? Where is the only remaining evidence that we are—were—a happy family?

I can't believe my parents. They are entirely erasing the past. Do they think that just taking down a few pictures will make me forget how great things used to be? Sure, the last year or so was not 100 percent fantastic, with all the screaming and fighting, but those three pictures were proof that my parents could get along. That we could be a family.

I think back to the discussion on the couch last night. I remember my father saying over and over again, "I just don't see us together." It made me so sad, because I see us together all the time. Why can't he just see us as a happy family?

Then I remember a different conversation I had a few days ago with Honey, when all the pictures were still in place. Maybe my parents just need a little help seeing it. Or maybe I do.

I pick up my cell phone and dial. "Honey's Kids," Honey says on the other end of the line.

"Hi, Honey. It's Cassie."

"Did everything go all right at the Seven Sails shoot?"

"Everything was fine," I tell her, using the most confident and self-assured tone I can muster. I absolutely hate lying to Honey, and I am about to tell her a whopper.

"I was just calling because . . ." I pause for a second. If there is any chance of turning back, now is the time, but I push on through.

"Because I got my school schedule wrong, and I

can actually go out for that spot you mentioned the other day. What was it again, some big campaign . . ." I trail off and act as nonchalant as possible. Like I can barely remember what the spot was for.

"Oh," Honey says excitedly. "The Happy Family Cruises? That's great. I think you're exactly what they're looking for. But wait." She stops talking. "Are you *sure* this won't conflict with summer school? I gave you all the dates, right?"

The dates completely conflict with summer school. The booking dates are the exact same time as the final presentations, but I *have* to try to book this commercial. It might be the only way for my family to see that we can be a happy family again. I know it's silly and doesn't make any sense, but it's what I have to do. I just feel it.

"I'm clear," I tell Honey.

"Well, okay. I'll see if I can get you a time slot, and I'll call or text you back."

I hang up and imagine my mom and dad watching me on TV as the words "Happy Family" scroll across my face.

CHAPTER 29

Honey had no problem getting me in for the Happy Family Cruises spot.

I'm early for my audition. Very early. I could have waited until the end of class and then raced up here for my appointment, and I probably would have still been on time. But telling Mr. Evans I had stomach cramps and was going to see the nurse and getting sent home meant I would not only definitely get here on time, but would also miss a substantial part of my stupid summer class. I know I told my parents I would faithfully attend summer school, but no one seems to be keeping their promises these days, so where is the harm in missing just part of one class? Of course, if I actually book this spot I'll have to figure out another plan, but for now just leaving class to go to this audition feels good. It feels like leaving the complicated, confusing part of my life behind for the camera-ready part.

It's been a week since they sat me on the couch and told me they were "moving forward with the divorce." I cried that night, but the next morning I made the decision not to let the situation have any effect on me. Ginger thinks I'm just being quiet, but really I'm just trying not to think about anything. That's my plan—to just not think about it. Okay, it's not a great plan, but at the moment the only thing I can do is *not* think.

My mom keeps asking me if I want to talk about it. I keep telling her, "No!" and going about my life as if nothing had ever happened. What's the point of talking about it with my mother? It's not like talking about it is going to change anything. If there was some magic phrase I could utter, a phrase that would make everything go back to the way it was when we all lived in the same apartment and did things on the weekends like regular families, I would have already said it. I think my mom was upset that I didn't have anything to say, but I really didn't, so what was I supposed to do?

At least if I can't be part of a perfect family in

real life, I can be part of one for thirty seconds.

As I walk up the stairs to the studio for my audition, I look at my watch and realize my summer class still has a few minutes until it ends. I picture everyone copying down the assignment for the next class while my desk remains empty. For a few seconds I feel guilty. I didn't like lying to Mr. Evans, and when Nevin showed actual concern for my well-being and offered to take notes for me I felt another pang of guilt, but it disappeared quickly. Maybe I would have felt worse if it had been more difficult to do, but faking my way out of class to get to this audition was just so easy. It was almost too easy.

When I get to the right floor and see the door for the casting office, I no longer feel even a little guilty. I know once I walk through that door I will be in another world. I won't have to worry about summer homework or chores or even think about the phrase "visitation rights." I can focus on saying the lines or brightening my smile or any number of things to make sure I am camera-ready.

I open the door and see about half a dozen girls in the room. A few of them have their mothers with them. I go to the sign-in sheet and examine the list of names. I see that Phoebe was here much earlier in the day, but it looks like I missed her.

I take a seat in the corner of the room and take my compact mirror out of my bag. I decided to wear just a tiny bit of makeup to this go-see. My parents forbid me from wearing any makeup at all, but they are so busy messing up our family that I don't think anyone will even notice a little bit of blush and some eyeliner. I hold the mirror up to my face and take out a tissue. I think my eyeliner is a bit too thick on my right eye, so I try to wipe some of it off, but the more I try to wipe it off, the worse it looks. I keep wiping and trying to make it look better, but I am on the verge of looking like a rabid raccoon. Why can't I do anything right?

I give up and go to the restroom. Luckily, I threw some makeup remover towelettes in my bag before leaving my house this morning. I gently move the cleansing pad under my eye, since I don't want to exchange eyeliner smudge for red irritation. I look at myself in the mirror and shake my head.

For a second I'm about to start thinking of all the stuff happening with my parents, but I point my finger at myself in the mirror and say out loud, "Cassie, stop it." I take a deep breath and examine

myself in the mirror one last time to make sure
I won't embarrass myself with any stray makeup
errors on camera.

I walk back into the waiting room and start
looking at the sides so I'll know what I'm doing
during my audition. It's a pretty simple spot. There
are four members of the happy family on the Happy
Family cruise: a dad, a mom, a son, and a daughter.
Each panel shows a different family member doing
something they enjoy. The dad practices his golf
swing, the mom is at the spa, the son is pigging
out at the pizza buffet with some friends he met
on the cruise, and the daughter is lounging by the
pool with some friends she met on the cruise. In
real life I would much rather be pigging out at the
pizza buffet, but I remind myself that, thankfully,
commercials are *not* real life. At the end of the
commercial the family spends the evening together,
having a meal in the fancy dining room. It's pretty
easy stuff, and since the waiting area has only girls
my age, I assume that we're going in together and
that they'll match families up later at the callback.

I am about to turn off my phone and prep for
my audition when it starts buzzing. The word DAD
flashes across the screen. I've been ignoring his

calls since the big announcement, and I consider just pressing ignore one more time, but something actually makes me answer. I dash around the corner for a bit of privacy and hold my hand close to my mouth as I talk.

"Hi, Dad," I say. Usually I'm overjoyed to hear from him, but at the moment my tone is glum at best.

"Hi, Peanut. I'm so glad you picked up. I've been trying you for days."

"I know," I say. My voice is devoid of emotion. I feel like a robot.

"I think we should talk," he says.

I don't say anything. Why does everyone want me to talk about this? I don't want to hear him tell me how everything is going to be fine and this has nothing to do with me. I know it has nothing to do with me. If it did, I wouldn't let it happen.

"Dad, I'm at an audition. I really can't talk now. I gotta go. Bye." I close my phone. It hurts to basically hang up on my dad. He was the one who took me on my first audition and convinced my mom that I should get an agent and everything. My mom has supported me in her own way, but my dad is the one who has encouraged me.

I decide to keep ignoring reality and go back to looking at the sides to prepare for my audition. These sides have a storyboard with them, showing exactly how they imagine the commercial will look. It shows the "happy family" just being happy. I try to imagine myself inside that commercial.

It would take very little to make me cry at this moment, but instead I turn off my phone and turn on the biggest, brightest commercial smile I have. I am going to book this spot and be part of this happy family if it kills me.

CHAPTER 30

I had a great audition. I never say I know I'm getting a callback, but this time I feel very strongly that I will. I walk out of the overly air-conditioned lobby onto the sun-baked street. It's a brutally hot day, and the sidewalks radiate heat. I feel the sweat beginning to bead across my forehead. I do not want to be a part of reality just yet. I want to hold on to this good feeling for as long as I can. I decide to go home and fill the bathtub with cool water and my favorite bubble bath and just forget about my enemy—reality—for a little bit longer.

By the time I get home I am covered in sweat. Before I start my bubble bath, I go to the refrigerator to get something cold to drink. I grab a can of diet soda and guzzle as much of it down as I can without choking. It hits the spot perfectly and immediately refreshes me.

Without even thinking, I run to the mirror in the bathroom. I want to remember exactly what this feels like and how it looks so I can remember this exact moment at auditions. I study myself in the mirror. My bangs are stuck to my forehead, and parts of my shirt are damp from sweat. I grab the can of soda and hold it up near my face like I would during a shoot. It's an incredibly unnatural position, but it's used all the time in commercials because it puts the person's face next to the product.

I take a sip of the soda and replicate the experience I had in the kitchen. I taste each drop of the liquid and experience the same level of enjoyment and refreshment that I did a few seconds ago, but this time I'm staring at myself in the mirror as it happens. I study the curve of my smile and pay attention to how my eyes crinkle.

This is me. This is Cassie enjoying something. This is Cassie enjoying a cold drink on a hot day. With each phrase I snap a mental picture of myself and try to burn the image in my mind.

Then I put down the almost empty can and take a deep breath in and out. I close my eyes tightly and then open them again so I can start with a blank slate. I put my hand around an imaginary can of soda and watch myself in the mirror. I pretend to take a sip from the pretend can and try to copy exactly how I looked when I was doing it for real. I make sure my mouth curves in the same way and that my eyes crinkle just enough. I freeze for a second and really study my expression.

Is this me? Is this Cassie enjoying something? I notice that my smile was a tad wider before and that I showed a few more teeth. I carefully make the adjustment until how I look in the mirror is how I look in my head. Yes. That's me. I finally recognize the copy of myself that I want to put out for the world to see, and I try to save it to the hard drive of my life.

The doorbell rings and breaks my concentration. I take the last sip out of the can, but this time I do it without even thinking about it or how it looks. I just want to finish the drink.

I walk through the living room and open the front door of the apartment. It's Ginger.

"Should we go to The Bench, or is it just too hot out? We could sit on the back fire escape and try to catch a breeze," she says.

I should have known Ginger would be waiting for me after class today. I haven't really seen her since the night I spent at her house after my parents told me the news. I know she wants to talk about it, but I don't really have anything to say. Ginger and I talk about everything, but I just want to forget what's going on in my real life for as long as I can.

"Actually," I tell her, "I was just about to take a bath."

I'm worried she'll be upset, but her face doesn't look hurt. She looks more concerned.

"Well, okay. It's no big deal. Call me when you're done with your bath, okay?"

"Ginger, I can't—" I say.

"Oh, do you have a go-see? Or did you get a callback for something?"

"It's not that," I say. How can I tell my best friend that I don't want to talk to her about the most devastating news in my entire life?

Ginger just looks at me sweetly. Not for a second does she suspect I'm trying to wiggle out of seeing her later. There's no way I can lie to her, so I say, "I have a lot of homework for my summer class."

Since Ginger is such a good student, homework is something she totally gets. "Oh, okay," she says, nodding her head. "I'll just see you later. You don't want to get behind in your class."

"Thanks, Ginger," I say. "You're the greatest."

She smiles and says, "No problem. That's what best friends are for. I'll see you later. Now go take that bath and finish your homework."

Ginger leaves, and as soon as she does I feel calmer but also a bit guilty. I'm sure I have homework I need to do for my class, so I totally told her the truth. The only part I fudged was my actual interest in doing that homework. I'm so far behind in class at this point that I don't think one afternoon of hard work is really going to catch me up. What's the point?

CHAPTER 31

After almost an hour of soaking, I look at my hands, and my fingers look like little raisins. The thick forest of bubbles has dwindled to a few floating islands of suds, but the water continues to be cool and soothing. I could stay here for a few more hours. I close my eyes and rest the back of my head against the spa pillow I have suctioned to the back of the tub. I am in my own little sanctuary, and nothing can disturb me.

Ding-dong. Ding-dong. The doorbell rings. Who can *that* be? My mom is still at work and would use her key, and Ginger knows I wanted to take a bath. It must be the mailman or something. I keep my eyes closed, assuming I can get back my quietude. *Ding-dong, ding-dong, ding-dong!* Again, only this time the pattern is faster and more insistent. What is wrong with this mail carrier? Can't they get the hint that no one is going to answer the door? Then again the doorbell, but this time it's accompanied by furious knocking. This is one persistent mail carrier. I yell from the bathroom, "O! K! I'm coming. Hold on!"

I step out of the bathtub and grab my plush terry-cloth robe. I put my hair in a towel and tighten the belt securely around my waist before stepping into my bath slippers. I walk to the door and check through the peephole, expecting to see some enormous package or at least a letter with some type of special delivery tag on it. Instead I see something totally different. Nevin!

I should just walk right back to my bath and ignore him, but I'm so angry that I actually swing open the door and just start yelling.

"What's wrong with you? I was in the middle of taking a bath, and you're ringing this bell like you're a deranged contestant on *Jeopardy!*'s Geek Week!" I shout.

"I'm sorry," Nevin says softly. He looks like I just punched him in the face.

Oh, why did I have to yell at him? He wasn't doing anything wrong. I change my tone and volume and say as nicely as I can, "It's okay. What do you want?"

"Well, I wanted to see if you were feeling any better."

"Yes, I feel fine," I tell him with a bit of defiance, and then I remember faking stomach cramps to get out of class today and add, "I think the bath I just had really helped." Then I remember I'm wearing a robe and that my hair is in a towel. "I really should go change," I tell him, trying to close the door.

"Of course, milady, but I wanted to make sure you had the notes for the quiz we have in class next week."

I halt closing the door immediately. "Quiz? What are you talking about?" I can feel the soothing calm the bath generated hitching a ride out of my body to make way for a village of panic.

"I think you might have missed Mr. Evans talking about it. He announced it a few times in class and then went over the material at the end. That's the part I think you missed, but I have the notes."

I suddenly remember promising my mom I would get at least a B-plus in this class. If I don't squeak by with at least a B, she will never let me go on another go-see until I'm ready for denture commercials. What am I going to do? It's not like my participation and homework grades are going to help me. I was planning on doing really well on the quizzes and stuff to sort of balance everything out, but if I can't do that, I'm pretty much doomed. The village of panic begins setting up shop in my body. What am I going to do?

Nevin is just standing there in the doorway as I imagine a terrible end to my summer. "I'm not doing anything now. If you want, we could go over the stuff together," he says.

"Yes!" I say. I don't even care that it's Nevin or that this means I have to actually study. I'm just grateful to have a way out of this particular predicament.

I pull Nevin into the apartment, sit him down at the dining room table, and say, "There are Cokes and soy things in the kitchen. Let me get changed and I'll be back in two minutes."

CHAPTER 32

I find it hard to believe that one person can hate the periodic table as much as I do. It is the stupidest thing I have ever come across, and after thirty minutes of studying my brain is totally fried.

"This thing doesn't make any sense," I say, pushing the book away from me.

"Curious you should say that, because it actually makes perfect sense. You see, it's all very logical. There are four groups—"

I stop Nevin before he launches into the different types of elements for, like, the tenth time since we sat down to study. "I need a break," I say, and get up from the table. I go over to the kitchen to grab a Juiced Up juice box. I booked a spot for them a few months ago, and the client was so happy with the commercial that he sent everyone involved in the production a case of juice boxes. I will be out of college before we finish them all. "You want one?" I ask Nevin, holding up a juice box.

"Yeah," he says, smiling and nodding his head. "That's a Juiced Up juice box. I saw you on the commercial for them just the other day when I was at my orthodontist waiting to get my braces tightened. You and some other girl are talking about how Juiced Up gives you energy to play soccer because it's infused with all these vitamins and herbal enhancements."

I hold up the juice box in the same way I did during the commercial and go into the little speech I had to say: "Juiced Up juice boxes aren't just juice, they're a whole box full of vitamins and super herbs. One box alone contains Vitamins A, B, and C, niacin, potassium, creatine, gingko, guarana, aloe, ginseng, lutein, and full day's supply of folic acid." The words roll off my tongue easily, and I say them in the same singsongy way that I did on camera, smiling and only taking a breath once in order to emphasize how complete the juice box is.

"That's amazing," Nevin says. It's nice to feel competent for five seconds instead of feeling totally overwhelmed by our science quiz. "But I don't understand."

"What don't you understand?" I ask, walking back over to the table and taking my seat across from him.

"I mean, all the commercials you do have so many, you know, words."

"Actually," I tell him, "we call that 'copy.' All the words in a script are called copy, and you're right. There was *a lot* of copy in that commercial, but what don't you understand?"

"Well, if I might impinge upon milady's kindness, why is it that studying science is so much more difficult than studying, as you call it, copy?"

"Well . . . ," I start to respond immediately, but then I realize I actually don't have a good answer. Why is it that science is so much harder? I probably memorize more copy in a week than in a whole grading period of science class.

"I don't know," I tell him. "I guess commercials just seem to make more sense. Like that Juiced Up commercial spot was a sporty spot. I was a soccer player, so a sporty spot means that I have to act a certain way versus, say, a spot for something serious like a new medicine or something."

"I see," he says, "so like the same way certain elements are part of a group. Like some are gases and some are solids." He takes the flash cards he made and starts grouping them together according to the type of element they are instead of just using the rigid structure of the periodic table. Suddenly I can see each of the elements not just as something made up to torture me but as something real. This is how I've always approached every audition I've ever been on. I try to make the words real for me, and I try to find ways to have them make sense for me.

"You see," Nevin continues, "hydrogen isn't just a gas. When it combines with oxygen you get—"

I finish the sentence for him, "You get H_2O, something real. You get water." Suddenly the elements are not just symbols. They are things, actually things that make up my life as much as anything else. "So if we take your cards and stop using the grid, we can find ways to organize them that makes sense to us and then put them back on the grid after that."

"Excelsior!" Nevin says.

"Oh, no. Is that an element? I don't remember that one."

"Uh, no. It is a Latin term used in Old English. It means, uh . . ." Nevin searches for the right phrase and then says, "You go, girl!"

Hearing something that might come out of a pop diva's mouth come out of Nevin's is like hearing Santa Claus curse. It's strange, and you want to unhear it, but it's also hysterical. I can't help laughing.

"Nevin, I think you should stick with Old English. It suits you better. Now, let's get all excelsior on this periodic table," I say, and open up our textbook to the place where we left off.

CHAPTER 33

"Oh, please. That's an easy one," I say, staring at the worn note card where Nevin has printed the letters for his collection of periodic table study aids. "'Ne' stands for neon. It's the gas commonly found in outdoor lighting. It's an inert gas, and the atomic weight is ten. It is odorless and colorless, and it goes here on the periodic table." I point to the eighteenth column on the second row.

"That's correct, milady."

After a whole afternoon of studying together, we have taken apart the periodic table and put it back together. It is no longer a jumble of strange letters and weird words. It's actually something that makes sense to me.

When I realize how long we've been sitting at the table, I get up and stretch. The strangest part is that the time has flown by. For the first time since last weekend I was completely focused on one task. I wasn't thinking about my parents or their news or even Rory and why he hasn't called me. I was just focused on studying and getting everything right, so the time flew by.

"You know what, Nevin? I think we deserve a treat. There should be some ice cream in the freezer."

"That sounds like a capital idea," Nevin says, using his pencil to punctuate his statement.

"I don't know what that means exactly, but I'm assuming it's good." I walk over to the freezer, but when I open it, I suddenly remember that I ate the last pint of Soy Ice we had the other night. "Looks like we're out," I tell him.

"Well it was a valiant attempt," Nevin says, looking a little disappointed. "Maybe next time."

"No way," I tell him. "We have earned a treat, and I'm going to get us one. Do you want to go down to Pinkadoodle on Mercer Street and get some frozen yogurt? My treat."

"With you? You mean, you and me go out in public where there are, you know"—he takes a deep breath—"other people around?"

"Yes, Nevin. Let me grab my purse." I grab my bag from the back of my chair and suddenly remember a detail that will make this outing much more pleasant. "One thing, Nevin. Can you lay off the milady stuff while we're in public? Just call me Cassie."

"Yes. Yes, of course, mi—," he starts off, but then immediately corrects himself. "Cassie." Poor Nevin.

"Great, let's go," I say.

I have a green tea yogurt with strawberries and Fruity Pebbles on top. Nevin also has green tea yogurt, but his has pineapple and carob chips on it. The heat from the afternoon has let up, and as the sun begins to set, a calm pink light embraces the city streets and a soft wind gently blows around us. We sit on the bench outside the store, quietly eating our yogurt. I realize how late it's getting and hope I'm not getting Nevin in trouble.

"Are your parents expecting you home for dinner?" I ask.

"No. My mom has her Pilates tonight, so it doesn't matter."

How could I be so stupid? Why did I say *parents*? I know his parents got divorced about two years ago and that his dad lives in Connecticut while Nevin lives in the city with his mom. I remember my mom telling me to be extra nice to Nevin while his family was going through the divorce. I also remember that advice going in one ear and out the other. I probably treated Nevin the same way I always treat him. How could I have been so cruel? And now here I am, putting my foot in my mouth and reminding him that he doesn't have parents. He has a mom and he has a dad. But he doesn't have parents. "I'm so sorry," I say.

"For what?" he asks, taking another spoonful of his yogurt.

"For saying 'parents' when I know you live with just your mom."

"Oh," he says. "That's okay. I don't really think about it. I mean not anymore. Not too much."

I don't say anything. I just stare down at my yogurt and watch it melt. A pink Fruity Pebble falls off the frozen part and joins a small puddle of melted yogurt and strawberry on the side of the cup. I never thought Nevin would be the person I would want to talk about this with, but here I am thinking about asking him questions and telling him things I wouldn't share with anyone else.

"So what was it like?" I ask.

Nevin puts his spoon in his yogurt. "You mean the divorce, don't you?" he asks, his voice quiet and soft. I nod my head slowly. "It was hard, but things are better now, and it's better than it used to be."

"What do you mean?"

"Well, before my parents were always fighting. I would come home from school and go right to my room to study or play a video game with headphones on, because they would be going at it in the living room, screaming and fighting and yelling at each other. That was the worst. That was worse than the divorce." Nevin talks like a regular kid for once. He doesn't use any of his Old English expressions, and even his voice is clearer and less nasal. "And there were some good things. Like when my dad remarried, I finally got a brother, even if José is only a step and thinks that *Star Trek: TNG* is superior to *Star Trek: Deep Space Nine.* Can you even imagine thinking that?"

I remember that Nevin's dad remarried a few months ago. His new wife is this very pretty, very young woman from the Dominican Republic named Mercedes. I can't even imagine one of my parents remarrying, let alone having a new sibling or even a step-sib. The very thought of those things terrifies me, so I just push them out of my mind. I can barely deal with even beginning to think about what might happen to my family.

"Do you miss your dad?" I ask, and wonder if I'm pushing Nevin too much. The divorce happened only a couple of years ago, and the ink is barely dry on the new marriage. I can't imagine it isn't still upsetting.

"A little bit." He pauses and then looks up at the large oak tree planted next to our bench. Then he adds, "Sometimes." Then finally he says, "Yes."

I look up at the oak tree also. The lights of the city filter through the tree's leaves and branches, and I decide to tell Nevin what I have been unable to tell anyone else.

"Nevin, my parents are getting a divorce." I spit each word of the sentence out of my mouth like seeds from a glass of orange juice.

Nevin puts his yogurt down on the other side of the bench and sort of smiles at me and nods his head with this knowing expression on it. He puts his hand on my shoulder but not in a creepy way. It's like he's just telling me he's there, and then he says the exact right thing to me.

He says nothing.

We just sit in the fading light of the summer with our half-eaten yogurts melting.

CHAPTER 34

"So," Mr. Evans says. "Let's get started on our little quiz."

Why couldn't my callback for Happy Family Cruises be this morning instead of this afternoon? At least then I would have a reason for skipping this quiz. Unfortunately, my afternoon call time means I will have plenty of time to take this quiz *and* go to the callback.

"Please put all your notes and materials either away in your backpack or under your desk and make sure your cell phones are turned completely off." He looks directly at me as his says this last part, and I just smile innocently like I have no idea what he's talking about. As soon as he looks in a different direction, I grab my cell phone out of my bag to make sure it is actually turned off.

I turn it over and see that I have one new text

message. Honey already confirmed me for the callback, and Ginger is at Chinese school. Mr. Evans is still shuffling some papers and organizing the quizzes, so I decide to take a second to see who it's from. Maybe my dad is texting me?

I click the keys to open the text and see:

HI MONIQUE! OK 2 TXT U? FINISHED A CALLBACK FOR CRUISE SPOT WANT 2 GO 2 USQ PARK W ME L8TR?

I gasp out loud, and everyone in class turns to look at me and not in a good way. I look from side to side, thinking of something to say to make everyone go back to what they were doing. Even Mr. Evans is looking at me with a frown and his hands on his hips. "Is everything all right over there, Cassie?"

"Uh, yeah," I say. "I just found a piece of bubble gum I'd been looking for in the bottom of my bag." I close my eyes, preparing for Mr. Evans to raise his voice, since I have just given him the stupidest excuse I've ever heard. Instead he says, "That reminds me: extra credit for anyone who can tell me what element from the periodic table is commonly found in bubble gum. Now let's get started."

I open my eyes, clear off my desk, shove my cell phone back into my bag, and take out a pencil.

I can't believe that Rory actually texted me. He wants to see me. I realize I should have texted him right back, but with Mr. Evans handing out the quiz, my cell phone is completely off-limits.

Once everyone has their quizzes, Mr. Evans announces, "Begin!" and starts walking around the classroom to make sure no one is cheating.

Everyone begins, and I know I should too, but I'm still thinking about the text from Rory. What exactly did it say? Did he say he was staying in the city or that he was going back home if I wasn't around? I know he wanted to go to the park, but was it with a bunch of kids or was it just with me? I take my pencil and try to write down the words I remember on the back of my quiz. I write down "USQ" and "callback," but then I draw a blank. If only I could take my cell phone out of my bag for, like, half a second I could see what he said.

"Cassie," I hear Mr. Evans's voice behind me. "If you want to have any chance of passing this quiz, you need to get started. Five minutes are already up, and you haven't even turned the paper over." Nevin hears this and snaps his head to look at me. He looks both confused and a bit annoyed.

"Oh, right," I say, and turn over the quiz. I look

at the clock on the wall. I have already lost a significant amount of time. I start bouncing my knee up and down, my nerves getting the better of me. I start reading over the questions. Shoot. Why did I get so distracted by my cell phone? Now my brain is all jumbled up, and the words on the page look familiar, but as I read through the questions, none of the answers really pop into my head.

I look around the room, and all the other kids have their heads bent over their papers and are furiously scribbling the answers to the questions. I just keep flipping through the pages of the quiz, hoping the answer to one of the questions will make itself known to me somehow.

I look over at Nevin, who is sitting across the room from me, and he catches me looking at him. Mr. Evans looks out the window, and Nevin puts down his pencil, then holds his palm out right next to his face and beams this strange and uncharacteristically bright smile at me. Then he goes back to his paper, so Mr. Evans doesn't see him looking up. What in the world was he doing? He looked like he was auditioning for some demented commercial!

Then it dawns on me. *It looked like he was auditioning for some commercial.* He is trying to remind me to use what I know from go-sees to help get me through the quiz.

I can do this. I think about each element and how when I was studying with Nevin I turned it into something real. I look back at the clock on the wall. I don't have that much time, but I'm able to answer at least the questions I know. The clock ticks down until there are only a few minutes left. I try to answer one last question before the end, but Mr. Evans calls out, "Time. Pencils down."

I drop my head on the desk, exhausted. My hand is cramped, and when I look over my quiz, I notice there are still questions I left blank, but at least the ones I answered I feel I got right. It's not an A but I'm also pretty sure I didn't fail.

Mr. Evans collects the papers and dismisses the class. I grab my bag to get my cell phone, but as I'm fumbling for it, Nevin comes over.

"I'm so glad you figured out my signal, milady. How did you do? I know you got the one on neon right, but I thought the question on hydrogen was a rather difficult and perplexing enigma. What thinkest thou?"

I'm barely listening to Nevin, since I'm trying to fish out my cell phone to read the text that Rory sent. Maybe there's still a chance I can meet him. "Yeah, yeah," I say to Nevin, and wave him away and walk out of the classroom. I look at my phone and see a new incoming text.

Once I'm outside the building, I punch the keys on my phone to see the new text.

GUESS MAYBE I MISSED U. C YA

Shoot. I can't believe I'm going to miss him. I text back:

HEY. HEADED TO USQ BEFORE MY CALLBACK ALSO. WHAT A COINCIDENCE. C U THERE.

I start running up Broadway. At first I am sprinting, and then I start sweating, so I take it down to a slow jog. Then I look at my watch and go back to my full-out run. When I am about a block away, I get another text from Rory.

COOL. C U SOON

Yes! He's still there. But now I'm looking like I just finished a triathlon. I duck into the Sephora store, which happens to be on my way. He knows I'll be there, so no reason to show up looking a mess.

Sephora is the perfect place to give myself a free mini makeover and dry off before seeing Rory. I normally don't use that much makeup, so I only need to get a little color smudge on my eyes to give a more dramatic effect to my usually wholesome features. Since I am there, I also decide to try out a new lip gloss. I pass over the all the fruity and smelly ones for something a bit more mature. I try a darker shade than I usually would, and after I apply it to my lips I have to say I think it looks good. I make a mental note to come back to the store later in the week to buy a whole tube of the gloss.

I stand in front of the full-length mirror next to men's cologne and sigh. Why do I have to look so plain? The smudged eye color and darker lip gloss help, but the truth is, I still look so ordinary. Honey always tells me that ordinary is a look that sells. "People look at you, and they see their sister or their best friend," she says. But today I want to look special.

The park is crowded but not unmanageable. I know most of the kids our age hang out by the area just north of the main pavilion, which is away from the crowds of people shopping for fresh berries or homemade cheese at the farmer's market. This side of the park is close to where a lot of the agencies and casting offices are, so a lot of the kids, and I assume some of the adults, hang out here between go-sees. I look around and see Brittany Rush. For a second I think about going over to say hi to her, but she's always scared me a bit, and we didn't get much closer at the Seven Sails shoot. She is absolutely beautiful and has booked more commercials than anyone I have ever heard of, but I haven't seen a lot of her on the circuit lately, and since I see she is with Phoebe's brother, Liam, I decide to leave them alone.

I continue to scan the crowd but still don't see Rory. I hope I didn't miss him because of that stupid quiz in my class. I walk around the outside loop of the park, since that will give me a good overview of the area. I try not to look too obvious, because I want to look as if I've just sort of shown up here on my own.

I circle the park twice. Nothing. I stop on the north edge again and sit on a bench and tie and untie my shoe about a dozen times, hoping he will just show up and catch me *not* looking for him but rather tying my shoe. Still no sign of him. I could text him again, but that seems like too much. I guess I'm not going to see him. I took too long at Sephora.

I look at my watch and realize I had better get

to my callback. I see that my shoelace is actually untied for real, and I bend down to tie it but realize there is something sticky on the bottom of my shoe. When I grab my foot to get a closer look, I put my hand in a sticky, disgusting piece of chewed gum. Yuck.

Then someone taps me on the shoulder.

CHAPTER 35

"Hey, Monique," a calm, soothing voice says. I don't even have to recognize the voice to know that it's Rory, since no one else would call me Monique. Because my one hand is covered in gum, I try to use my other hand to pull some of the mess off of me before sitting back up and saying hi. But instead of releasing the gum, I have simply spread the sticky goo to both hands, which are instantly joined together as if stuck mid-clap.

"Hi, Rory," I say as naturally as possible, ignoring the fact that my hands are in an incredibly unnatural position. He must think I'm practicing to be a trained seal.

Rory gives me a strange look and says, "I hope I'm not bothering you. Were you . . . uh . . . praying?" The inflection in his voice makes me think he's not even sure if he has the right word, but seeing me bent over with my hands strangely clasped together, what else would he think?

"You aren't bothering me at all." I quickly pull my hands apart and stuff them in the front pockets of my jeans. I feel the rubbery glue sticking to the inside of my pants, and for a second I wonder how I will ever get them out. "I was just hanging out before my callback."

"Cool," he says, and smiles at me. His smile is a thing of beauty. "What's your callback for? Is it Happy Family Cruises?"

"Yeah, it's over there," I say before realizing that I should not have said something that needed a gesture to go with it. I sort of use my elbow to indicate the general direction. I'm sure Rory thinks I am having a spasm.

"That's so awesome. I just had my callback this morning. I can walk you there." I pause for a moment; as my hands are permanently attached to my pockets, it makes going from sitting to standing a bit more difficult than I imagined. Somehow I do it without losing my balance, although the possibility of falling over on the sidewalk is not out of the question.

I follow Rory out of the park, and we start walking toward the casting office. We are walking side by side, so I have to use my peripheral vision to look at him. The thing about Rory is that he always looks the same, like he just stepped off a set. His brown, slightly shaggy hair is always perfect, his slightly tanned skin is always perfect, his just-got-out-of-soccer-practice clothes are always perfect. He has this smile that is dazzling, but he clearly knows how to use it. He'll look very serious for a few seconds and then all of a sudden laugh at a joke he just made, and there is this explosion of teeth and charm.

We have been walking for a few blocks when I realize Rory has been doing all the talking. I don't really mind, because it means I don't have to talk at all. He's not grilling me about my feelings about the divorce or asking what I am going to do when my dad moves to California. He's not ruining this perfectly lovely walk to my callback with a lot of hard questions about my real life, and that's fine by me.

We finally get to the building where the callback is, and Rory is still talking. I like to watch the way his lips almost bounce off each other as he talks. Maybe everyone's lips do this, but on Rory it is particularly charming.

"Well, this is the place," he says. I nod but don't say anything.

"Hey," he says, suddenly very excited. "Did you know that they're gonna shoot the commercial on the actual boat and not on some set?"

"Really?" I ask, finally uttering a sound.

"Yeah. It's going to be docked in the Hudson River at one of those piers on the West Side. Isn't that cool?"

"Totally," I say, wondering when I will move beyond one-word sentences.

"I guess it's lucky I got the right callback," he says, and his usually open smile subtly changes to more of a grin, prompting me to go into full sentences once again.

"What do you mean, 'right callback'?" I ask. *How can you get a wrong one?* I wonder.

"Well . . . ," he says, turning his face away. "I got called backed for one of the cruise passengers. It would have been weird if I had gotten called back for the brother and you were being called back for the sister . . . because then it would have been weird. . . ."

"What would have been weird?" I ask, not sure what he is getting at.

"Well," he says, looking down at the ground. "There's something I've been wanting to ask you."

CHAPTER 36

Inside my brain I am shouting, Ask! Ask! Ask! but outside I just calmly look at him and say, "What did you want to ask me?" I smile and flip my hair from one shoulder to the other.

Rory looks up and says, "I wanted to see if you would go with me and a few friends to hear a band in the park on Saturday, and if we were playing brother and sister it would be weird." He laughs this fun, flirty laugh that shows he is maybe a little bit nervous. "So what do you say? Do you want to go?"

"YES!" I shout with way *way* too much enthusiasm. I try to remain calm and cover with a more neutral but affirming, "Sure. That sounds like fun."

"Then it's a date," he says, and starts walking away. "Oh and break a leg on your callback. It would be awesome if we were both on that big cruise ship."

"Thanks," I say. The sweat from my palms has released my hands from their pocket jails, and I use one to wave good-bye to Rory as he walks away.

I have a *date* with Rory. I can't believe it. I truly can't believe it. Rory is so perfect. He is more than perfect—he's totally "camera-ready." Finally something in my real life doesn't totally suck. Now if I can just book this Happy Family spot, I'll have a perfect social life and a perfect family. Granted, one of them is only on TV, but for now that's as close as I'm going to get.

I take the elevator up to my callback. I sign in immediately and realize I am actually a few minutes late. Luckily, there are so many people in the waiting room I don't think anyone really notices. A casting assistant hands me back the size card I filled out at the original audition and says, "We're typing out today, so don't leave until I have you checked out."

"No problem," I say. Usually at a callback you go in, get on tape, and leave, but sometimes they want to see how you look with other people, so they might call you in with one person and then try you out with another. You can't leave until you're checked out, so it can take a while.

As I wait to get called in, I look around the room and enjoy the mix of fake and real families. In some cases there is a girl or boy about my age at the callback with his or her real parent. You can spot the real parents right away, because they look like the parents you might see on the street or at the supermarket. They just look normal. The other combination is a commercial mom or dad who is at the callback with one of their real kids. You can spot these parents right away too, as they are perfectly groomed and poised. The moms are pretty and the dads are handsome. Their real kids are bored and unruly, unlike the fake kids who are anxious and preparing. It's a strange brew.

"I need the following four people in the studio," a young casting assistant says, looking down at his clipboard. He reads my name last, and I follow the others into the room. We stand in front of the camera while about half a dozen people sit on the other side of the camera inspecting us. Of course, no one looks directly at us. They all look at the monitor to see how we look on camera. What we look like in person has little to no bearing on the matter. I remember when I first started going out on auditions how weird it was to be standing three feet from someone and have them stare at my image on the screen rather than at me, but I quickly realized how you look on camera is more important than how you really look.

"Can you line up in this order? Father, mother, son, daughter. Let's get a clean slate for each of you when I point."

The camera lights flash on and the assistant points at the dad, who steps forward and says his name and agency. The assistant shouts, "Profile," and he turns left and right, showing each side of his face. We each go through the exact same dance, and then we wait. I just stand there and smile and try not to look nervous or bored. I think about Rory, and that makes it easy to smile.

For the next twenty minutes it's like a game of human Scrabble, where the tiles are endlessly rearranged. Sometimes I am with the same brother and two different parents or the dad stays the same and the mom and brother change or the whole family changes. Finally the perfect family takes shape. They seem to settle on me as the daughter with the same brother and dad, but they keep changing out the mom until my old friend Ashley Pruitt walks in.

I mouth a very excited, "Hello!" to her and

wave, and she does the same exact thing back to me. I didn't see her in the waiting area, so I guess she just showed up. She gets in line but grabs my hand and squeezes it before turning toward the camera to slate.

Once they have all four of us together, everyone behind the camera seems to nod and smile. The director walks up to us and says, "Looks like a happy family to me. You're all dismissed. Thanks for your time."

A happy family indeed.

CHAPTER 37

"How do you think you did on the quiz?" Nevin asks as he walks across the courtyard.

I am still deep in my daydream about Rory and my callback. The very word "quiz" is like having a bucket of fried chicken thrown in your face. I sigh audibly, realizing that once I'm home there's no way to avoid reality.

"Nevin," I say. "Can we *not* talk about the quiz right now?" I just want to hold on to my daydream a little longer.

"Sure," he says, and follows me into the building. "Anyway, I really wanted to ask you something else."

"Fine," I say, "but let me just get upstairs and wash my hands." They are still a little sticky from the gum situation earlier. Nevin follows me into the apartment, and I go right to the sink to really scrub off the goo. As soon as I get off the last bit, I turn off the water and the phone rings.

"Do you want me to get it?" Nevin asks.

"Let me just dry my hands. I'll do it." I grab a towel and look at the caller ID. I don't recognize the number, so I just pick it up and say hello.

"I'm looking for Professor Herold. Is she available?" a female voice asks.

"That's my mom. Can I take a message?"

"Yes, please. I already left her a voice mail on her cell phone, but please tell her that we had to reschedule her appointment with Ms. Bueno because she was called into court for a case she's working on. Can I give you the new information?"

I grab a pen and notepad from the kitchen counter and write down all the information and hang up.

"I wonder why my mom has an appointment with a lawyer," I say out loud, forgetting that Nevin is waiting for me.

"Oh," he says, and looks down. "I guess it's . . . the . . ."

"The what?" I ask. I truly have no idea what he is talking about.

"Well, it might be your mom's . . ." He stops midsentence as if he is gathering some courage and then says, "Divorce lawyer."

The words pierce my heart.

"I think I overheard my mom talking to your mom the other day, asking for a recommendation, and Ms. Bueno was my mom's lawyer so . . ."

My face turns red and my eyes tear. Of course it's for the divorce. I've done a good job blocking the whole thing from my mind over the past few days. It was one thing to hear my parents say they were getting a divorce. It's another thing to be taking messages from lawyers who are about to tear my family apart. I pick the piece of paper with the message on it off the counter and start ripping it into little pieces as the tears fall down my face.

Nevin doesn't say anything. He doesn't tell me to stop. He just quietly watches as I turn the information into confetti.

Finally Nevin says, "I hid car keys."

"What?" I ask, wiping the last few tears off my face.

"I hid car keys. My dad would leave at night to go visit his new girlfriend after they told me about the divorce, and I would hide his keys so he couldn't leave. It would stop him from leaving that night, but that was about it."

I look down at the small pile of confetti and wonder how many notes, legal papers, and letters I would have to tear up to stop this from happening. It would be a mountain.

"The thing is, I knew it wouldn't stop the divorce from happening. I mean, who stays married just because they can't find their keys?" Nevin does his weird snorty laugh, but it doesn't bother me at all. Instead I actually find it comforting. "I just did it because it felt like something I could do. I bet it felt good tearing up that note."

I nod. "It did." I think I finally get what he's trying to say. "It felt like I had control for just a few seconds."

"Good for you," he says, and smiles at me. I smile back. Nevin has been the one person I've been able to talk to about the whole horrible mess that is my family, and it's not just the fact that he has been through it that makes him easy to talk to. Being with Nevin feels easy. I don't have to worry about what I say or how I act. I'm about to thank him for being so understanding when there's a rapid knock at the door. I give my face a final wipe of my hand so whoever it is won't know I've been crying.

I open the door and it's Ginger. "Did he tell you the good news?" she asks, unable to control her excitement.

"What good news?" I ask.

"Well, I was about to ask you," Nevin says. "My dad has rented that house at the Jersey shore that we used to all go to when we were kids. Remember?"

"Yeah," I say, thinking about the crazy sand castles we used to build with moats filled with ocean water and spires topped with tiny shells. We went there a couple of times as kids and loved every second of playing in the cool ocean water during the day and playing games on the deck at night.

"Well, we're going the week after our summer class gets out. . . ."

"And my Chinese school," Ginger adds.

"Right, and my dad will be there with my stepmom and my stepbrother José, and he said I could invite you and Ginger like when we were kids. Would you like to celebrate the end of class at the beach?"

"Doesn't that sound awesome?" Ginger asks.

A week away from the city relaxing near the

ocean and wiggling my toes in the warm sand sounds spectacular. "Actually, it does. It sounds totally awesome," I say.

"Thank you so much for inviting us, Nevin," Ginger says.

"Thanks, Nevin," I say, but I hope he knows I'm thanking him for more than just the invitation.

CHAPTER 38

"Ginger it's just a group date," I say for maybe the hundredth time.

"All the other words in that statement do not matter one bit. The only word that has any importance is the last one. DATE."

"Oh, no," I say, and flop down on her bed over the layers and layers of clothes I have been trying on all afternoon. "When you say it like that, it makes the butterflies return." I put my hand over my stomach just to emphasize the strange feeling I have. "Why don't you come with me?"

"No way. I know us. You'll spend the whole time talking to me and never have any time alone with him."

"Oh, I guess you're right," I say, and grab whatever garment is lying next to me and use it to cover my face.

"Cassie, you go on bookings where your face is seen by millions of people, and that never makes you nervous."

"Yeah, but I'd rather be in front of a million strangers than one boy I actually know and *like*." I pull myself off the bed and stand in front of the full-length mirror in Ginger's room.

Why in the world is Rory interested in me? I'm not the prettiest girl he sees at auditions, and I'm not the funniest or smartest. I can't think of a single thing I have done or said around him that makes me very interesting. Mostly when we're together we're either auditioning or he's talking. Maybe just liking him so much is enough for him to like me back.

"Okay," Ginger says very seriously. "We only have a little bit of time left before you have to go and meet him." She grabs the two finalists I've brought over from the hook behind her door. "It's between this . . ." She holds up a bright blue tiered skirt made of a lacy cotton fabric with a matching blue T-shirt that has some sequins decorating the front. I look at the outfit as she holds it in front of my body. It's exactly the type of thing you should wear on a group date to hear a band with a boy you like. It's fun and flirty and has a bit of a sophisticated feel to it.

"Or this," Ginger says, and the other candidate appears beneath my neck. It's a pink floral print dress that is made of a sheer cotton fabric, with tiny straps that tie behind the neck. The hemline is below the knee, and the skirt is full and bouncy.

"I love this dress," I tell Ginger, admiring the delicate flowers in the mirror.

"Finally, you'll wear the dress," Ginger says.

"No!" I say. "I think I'll wear the skirt and T-shirt."

"But you just said you love the dress. And it's *totally* you, Cassie."

"I know, but . . ." I trail off. I guess I want Rory to see the girl he expects to see tonight. The girl who would get the part playing this girl on TV.

Ginger takes the dress from me and hands me back the hanger with the T-shirt and skirt. "You know what? You can save this dress for the beach. That skirt will be perfect for walking on the board-walk because it will catch the breeze, and that color will go great with a tan."

I look at the dress and realize she's right. "I wonder if that place we used to go to as kids that's kind of fancy is still there. I could wear it there."

"Oh, you mean the Starfish Grill. I love that

place. Remember when we got our very first Shirley Temples there, but when they made one for Nevin they called it something else?"

"Oh, yeah. They called it a Roy Rogers," I say, remembering that evening a few years back when we were still in elementary school.

"Nevin swore they tasted different even though they were exactly the same."

"I remember," I tell her, and think about how Nevin used to crack us both up back then.

"You can save that dress for the Starfish Grill. It will be perfect, and I'll wear my pink maxi dress too."

"That's awesome." I love when we match clothes. We haven't done it in years, but it will be fun to go back to it at the beach. "Maybe we can get Nevin to wear one too," I say, and Ginger laughs her funny little giggle that sounds almost like she's sneezing.

"Oh, and I've been waiting to tell you something about our trip to the beach."

"Yeah, what?" I ask, taking the T-shirt from her and smoothing out the fabric with my hand.

"Well, I was chatting with Ming-wei the other day, and . . ."

"And . . . ," I say, excitement building in my voice.

"Oh, it's not that big a deal, but it turns out that he'll be at the Jersey shore the same time we are. He'll be just a town away from us."

"WHAT?" I shout, throwing the T-shirt on the bed and jumping up and down to show my excitement. "That's awesome! Not a big deal? Are you crazy? That is a huge deal," I tell her.

Ginger bites her lip and wrinkles her forehead. "It *is* a big deal, isn't it? If I see him, it will be the first time I'll have any interaction with him outside of class. You know, in real life."

"Don't worry. I'll be there the whole time," I say, and put my arm on her shoulder.

"That's what I was hoping you'd say," Ginger says, and she put her arm around me. "You better get changed if you still want me to do your hair like that picture I showed you online."

"Thanks, Ginger." Sometimes having a best friend in charge of wardrobe, hair, and makeup is better than any professional in the world.

CHAPTER 39

Five. That is the number of words Rory has spoken to me since I've been at the concert. Specifically he said, "Hey babe. Glad you're here," when I first arrived. Then he went to hang out with some guy friends, and then five minutes later the band started. They have now been playing for forty-five long, ear-deafening minutes.

The only word I can use to describe this band is LOUD. I stand on the edge of the crowd, far enough away from Rory that he can't have a conversation with me, but not so far away that he can't glance at me every now and then. I try to make sure that when he looks over I appear like I'm really enjoying the music. I move my hips and head to the beat (if you can call it that), and sometimes when I'm sure he's looking over at me, I close my eyes so it looks like I'm really connecting to the music. Actually, when I have my eyes closed I'm praying that each song will be the last song we have to endure. There are car alarms that sound better than this band. Seriously, I'd rather have someone beat my ears than listen to this band.

However, I seem to be in a minority. This girl taps me on the shoulder and screams, "They're amazing. What's their name?"

Rory told me their name, but the relentless sound has drained any memory of it from my brain. I think it's some name related to food, but I scream back, "I DON'T KNOW."

Then the girl says, "IDA'S TOE?"

"NO," I scream. "I DON'T KNOW!"

She nods her head and screams, "THANKS!" Then she puts both arms in the air and screams, "IDA'S TOE ROCKS!"

I remember in that moment that I have an Aunt Ida and that I've seen her feet. They are nothing to celebrate.

At one point Rory looks over at me and waves. I wave back and smile just a bit. It's my commercial smile and not my real smile. I wonder which of his smiles he's using. Then he mouths something and gives me the thumbs-up sign. I shake my head and squint my eyes, indicating that I'm not sure what he's saying. He puts his thumb up and mouths the phrase again, only this time it is much slower. The second time I think the first word is "I." Then he does it again, and I think he's saying, "I love you." I practice saying the phrase to myself, and all the movements fit.

Freeze everything.

What am I supposed to do? Rory has just told me he *loves* me on our *first* date. That is insane. It's too much. It's too fast. I'm not sure how I feel. Sure I like him, but *love*?

I keep my mouth sealed tightly but give him a thumbs-up. I figure that's the best compromise until I decide how I feel. The band announces their last song, and despite the fact that my ears are ringing, I want them to keep playing, because once the show is over I know Rory and I will have to talk to each other, and what am I supposed to say to a boy who has just told me he loves me? Well, actually, he mouthed it, or at least, I think he mouthed it.

As I suspected, the band stops, and Rory starts walking over to me, nodding his head and mouthing, "I love you," over and over again with his thumb up. Oh, this is too much! I can't believe this boy is declaring his love for me with so much enthusiasm. I just put my thumb up and nod.

He gets closer and closer, and only when he's directly in front of me do I realize the depth of my stupidity. I can actually hear him saying, "Olive Juice! Olive Juice!" and I instantly remember the name of the band. He wasn't telling me he loves me. He was just saying the band's name.

When will I learn that things are not always what they appear to be?

CHAPTER 40

After the concert everyone decides that it would be cool to walk along the path by the Hudson River. My curfew is not for another hour, so I have plenty of time to make it home. As the group moves en masse from the park where the concert was held across town to the river, the couples slowly begin to peel off like some kind of urban square dance. At one point we are two groups, girls and boys, and then as we arrive at the water we are about half a dozen boy-girl couples. Now the night begins to feel like a date, or at least what I think a date should be like, since I've never actually been on one.

Even though it's night, the moon gives off enough light so you can make out the edges of the few clouds that hang in the sky. Once we get to the river, the expanse of the sky opens up, and I am reminded once again that Manhattan is actually an island. We start walking down the path along the river, and Rory is still talking about the band.

"The thing that is so awesome about Olive Juice is that they play all different types of music."

"Yeah," I say, even though I couldn't really tell one song from the other. It all just sounded like static to me. For a second I consider telling Rory this. Why shouldn't I? It's what I really think, but when I look over at him and his sweet smile and sunburnt cheeks I change my mind. Why ruin this moment with what I really think? Do I really owe anything to reality? What has it ever done for me?

I listen to Rory as we walk along the water and then something unexpected happens. He asks me a question. "So what's up with you?"

I have no idea how to respond. I was really getting into a listen groove, so responding feels strange and alien at the moment. I don't know what to say. We walk in silence for a few steps, and the seconds pass like pushing a giant boulder up a hill. I tell myself to say something. Say anything.

Then something truly terrible happens. I start to think about Nevin and how easy it is to talk to him. How he's the only person I've really talked to about all the stuff that is going on with my family.

Then I make a conscious effort to move Nevin out my mind.

"Everything is great," I finally say. "I'm having this totally awesome summer just hanging out with my friends and my family. I just like having fun and chilling." Of course I hear the words coming out of my mouth, but I really don't believe that I'm speaking them. I sound like a complete idiot. Where did I come up with this? Who talks like this? Actually. I know exactly who talks like this. Commercial Cassie. What I just said sounds like an ad for me rather than plain old me. Not to mention that it couldn't be further from the truth.

"That's cool," Rory says, and then points out over the water. "Look, a cruise ship." Out in the distance I see a gleaming white rectangle with soft, glowing lights. "Hey, have you heard anything about the Happy Family Cruise spot?" he asks. Another question, but this one I can answer.

"No," I say.

"Me either, but it shoots in, like, a few days so we better find out soon."

"Oh," I say, realizing that at least not booking the spot means I will be able to go to the science museum and complete my final.

"Yeah," Rory says. "I'm glad it's not next week, because that week my family goes to our house in the Hamptons."

"You have a house in the Hamptons?" I ask, even though he just said he did. It's clear that my mind and my mouth are not on the same team tonight.

"Yeah, it's amazing. It's only a few blocks from the beach, and we have this saltwater pool."

"It sounds great," I say. I've never been to the Hamptons, but I've always wanted to go. Once I had a callback for a commercial that was scheduled to shoot in the Hamptons, but I didn't book it.

"Maybe you should come for a day that week. It's easy to take the train, and my mom could pick you up and drop you off at the station on, like, Wednesday when she's not playing tennis."

Is this an invitation? It sounds like an invitation. It's not a concrete invitation, but he is inviting me. Isn't he?

"I'd like that," I say, and even though we're walking side by side I can tell that Rory is smiling. Then suddenly our arms that have been swinging next to each other brush against each other, but instead of moving farther away from me or giving me more room, Rory moves closer. He stops walking for just a second, takes my hand very gently, and then continues walking along the river.

We are walking and holding hands. No one is around to yell, "CUT!" and that's fine with me.

CHAPTER 41

I check my watch before turning the key in the lock on the apartment door. I am a full seven minutes early for my curfew. I don't want this feeling to end, so I consider walking around the block before heading home, but I figure coming home early will score me points for when I tell my mom I want to go to see a boy she doesn't know in the Hamptons for a day. I'm sure his parents will call and work out the details, but for now all I can think about is a day in the Hamptons.

I open the door, expecting all the lights to be off, but instead every lamp is turned on and my mom is standing in the middle of the living room.

"Cassie, did you have a nice time with your friends?" she asks.

"Yeah, it was great," I say. I take a few more steps

into the apartment and realize empty cardboard boxes are everywhere. I assume they're going to be used for some new craft project. But tonight even my mom's obsession with crafting doesn't bother me.

"Did you like the band? What was their name again? Uh . . . Orange Juice or something?"

"Olive Juice," I say, and remember the silly mistake I made with Rory. I'm grateful that now it's just a funny story. I tell my mom about how horrible the band was, and she laughs at my description of their performance. Then I tell her how we took a walk along the water, and she listens to every word I say. She's good at listening when it's important. She doesn't ask a lot of prying questions, and she respects my privacy. I want to tell her about being invited to the Hamptons, but it suddenly hits me that our apartment is *full* of empty boxes. "Mom, what *are* all these?"

"Cassie," my mom says, and sits down on the couch. "I've been trying to talk to you about this for a while. Sit down next to me."

I take a seat next to her and say, "You've been wanting to talk to me about boxes?"

"Not exactly. Look, you're not a baby anymore.

You're growing up, and I need to have a mature conversation with you."

I immediately put my head down and stare at the floor. Why is it that "growing up" is always on grown-ups' terms? It's like, when I want to do something, I always get told I can't because I'm *not* old enough, but when my mom wants me to act mature, it's for something she wants me to do.

I don't look at her. I keep staring down.

"These boxes are for your dad." She pauses. I can tell she's waiting for me to have a reaction, but I don't. I just keep staring down at the wooden floor. "He's coming to move his stuff out so he can get his own place." Another pause, but I don't blink. "After the . . . divorce."

There's the word I was waiting for. It's like a light switch. The moment I hear it, I turn off. I don't want anything to do with it.

"Look, Mom. I've got to study with Nevin tomorrow for our big final at the science museum. I better get to bed." I go to get up from the couch, and my mom gently puts her hand on my thigh.

"Cassie, you can't run away from this. It's happening. I'm sorry it is. It's hard for me, too, but

I need you to understand what's going on."

I don't say anything. I continue to stare at the floor.

"I know you think we're pretty different, Cassie, but I'm worried we're actually too much alike."

"What do you mean?" I mumble, my gaze not leaving the floor.

"Look, I know you love going out on auditions and booking spots, but I worry that it's too much of a distraction from living your real life. When I was your age, I was the same way."

"You wanted to be in commercials?" I can't even imagine my mom wanting that.

"Oh, no. Not in that way. I've always loved numbers and equations. But Cassie, I realized I sometimes love a good mathematical problem and pay more attention to it than other things because it's something I know I can solve if I work really hard at it. For me, math is an escape from reality, and lately I've started to think I rely on it too much. I worry you use commercials in the same way."

For a second, just a mere second, I take in what she says, and then I push it out of my mind. I fake a huge yawn and then stretch and cover my hand with my mouth. This time she can't stop me.

"Mom, no problem. I get it. I understand. I'm just really tired." I get up off the couch without looking at her. I walk directly to my room and close the door behind me. I'm not about to let reality get a hold of me tonight when I have to start planning for my day at the beach with Rory next week.

CHAPTER 42

Sunlight pierces through the blinds in my room as I slowly open my eyes. The level of brightness makes me think I am either going to be very late for class or I've missed it altogether. I reach my arm over my head to turn the face of my alarm clock toward me and confirm that even if I leap out of bed immediately, I will still be very late for class.

For a brief moment my biggest concern is a tardy mark in my summer class. I try to hold on to the half-conscious state for as long as I can, but then I begin to remember the reality of my life and all its complexities. Worrying about a tardy mark seems blissful by comparison.

I pull my blanket over my head, but the sunlight still penetrates the fabric. After a minute the air under the covers begins to feel heavy and thick. I want to stay hidden in my bed, but the physical need for fresh air forces me to pull the covers off my face, and in that moment I make a decision.

"That's it!" I say out loud. "Enough!" I just can't take it anymore. I feel like this statue I've seen at Rockefeller Center of this man with the shape of a body builder struggling to hold up a globe on his back. His face is twisted in anguish, and his arms seem to shake from the pressure. I'm going to deal with reality and throw that globe off my back. I get out of bed, grab the cord to the blinds, and pull so hard that they almost snap off the window frame. Sunshine fills the room, and the intensity of the light makes me squint, but I feel determined. I will accept the fact that no matter how perfect my life is at a go-see, the reality is that my parents are getting a di—

My cell phone vibrates underneath my pillow. I shove my hand under my pillow and grab my phone. There are six missed calls, and I see that Honey is calling.

"Hello," I croak into the phone, sounding like I've been asleep for days.

"Cassie, kiddo, this is my third call this morning." Well, that accounts for half my missed calls. "Where are you? Never mind. It doesn't matter. What matters is where you're going!"

"What?" I'm not sure whether I'm still half-asleep or whether Honey is not really making any sense.

"Cassie, you booked the Happy Family Cruises spot. Do you realize how *huge* this is? They plan to run this spot both national and international. They'd probably air them on Mars if they knew how to."

"This is . . ." I'm not sure how to finish the sentence.

"FANTASTIC!" Honey shouts, finishing the sentence for me. "Cassie, you *are* the Happy Family daughter."

Actually, I'm the exact opposite, but if I accept this booking it means I will indeed be her for at least one day.

CHAPTER 43

I accept the booking and go back to sleep.

By the time I actually get out of bed I realize it's too late to go to class for any reasonable amount of time. I decide to do some damage control and head out to Solazzo's Bakery to buy some protection. Surely a few of their delicious cannoli will help me tell Ginger and Nevin that I'm going to the Hamptons instead of the Jersey shore. Of course, it might take more than cannoli to smooth things over with Nevin, since booking this spot means I won't be at the final for our science class, but I'll just deal with that when the time comes.

From two blocks away I can see the line in front of Solazzo's. It wraps around the block and stretches for at least another full block, and people seem to keep joining it. But this line *isn't* for Solazzo's Bakery. It's for the Pretty Perfect Cupcake Café, which opened about a year ago. It was featured on a reality TV show, because the owner of the bakery is this very pretty young woman who loves to scream at her staff behind the scenes but is all smiles and giggles at the counter. The cupcakes are smothered in a garden of brightly covered flowers and are featured at events like celebrity weddings.

A few months ago Ginger and I put on dark glasses and waited in line just to see what all the fuss was about. We didn't want Mrs. Solazzo to see us patronizing her biggest competitor. I don't think we even came close to finishing the cupcakes. The icing tasted like eating sugar right out of the box. The cake was dry and resembled sawdust more than anything edible. One bite and we tossed them away, vowing never to stray from the chocolate-covered cannoli at Solazzo's Bakery, where we've been going since we were kids. I know the cupcakes from Pretty Perfect look, well, both pretty and perfect, but they taste pretty awful. What's the point of a cupcake looking so nice if it tastes so bad?

I walk right past the line for Pretty Perfect and all the people waiting in it. Pretty Perfect is a fantasy of what a bakery in New York City should be. They see the place on TV and think that means it's good or something. All those people in line are in for a disappointment. It's a shame they don't know that the good stuff is actually not what they see on TV but in the cozy little bakery right next door.

I push open the door to the Italian bakery, which has been on the block for more than a hundred years. It's busy but not nearly as crazed as Pretty Perfect. As soon as the register rings at Pretty Perfect you are shown the door so the next customer can purchase the same exact thing. At Solazzo's it's the opposite. Every customer is encouraged to relax with an espresso or an Italian soda at one of the small café tables.

"Hello, Miss Cassie," Auntie Sofia says from behind the counter when I walk in.

"Hi, Auntie Sofia," I say. All the kids in the neighborhood call her Auntie Sofia. She started working at her family's bakery during the Depression, when she was just a kid. She has got to be the oldest person I know, but she is also one of the quickest. I have seen her slice a tart, frost a cake, make a cappuccino, and ring up a customer all at the same time. Her head barely peeks over the top of the glass counter. Her hand reaches around the side, holding a small biscotti. "Here you go. Taste this while I finish with Mrs. Baumann." I take the crumbling cookie from her hand and put it directly into my mouth. Of course, it's delicious.

When she finishes with the customer before me, she asks me what I need today, and I tell her three chocolate-covered cannoli.

"Three?" she asks. "Well, one for you and one for Miss Ginger, but who will be getting the third?"

"Actually," I say, "it's for Nevin."

She smiles and nods. "Oh, I see. That Nevin is such a nice boy. Don't you think so?"

Everyone is always telling me how nice Nevin is. Usually I just ignore it, but for some reason today I say, "Yes, he is." I think about how he's been the only person I've felt comfortable talking to about the divorce and how he's helped me in class and how he's always ready to listen to me. For a second a pang of guilt washes over me, but I put it out of my mind.

Auntie Sofia places the chocolate tubes with creamy filling in a box, and then uses some red-and-white-striped string to tie the lid shut. I walk out of the bakery past the line in front of Pretty Perfect, and I actually feel bad for all those people. I know the cupcakes from Pretty Perfect are the stars of the most popular food reality show, but they can't compare to the treats from my own local bakery just next door.

CHAPTER 44

I sit on a bench in the shade across from the kids' playground in the building courtyard with the box of cannoli on my lap. Ginger and Nevin should be coming home any minute now. As I wait, I watch the kids playing on the seesaw. I remember the very first day I met Ginger on the seesaw. She was with a chubby man with a bright red beard, who turned out to be her dad. When she ran over to him, I was totally confused because I had never met someone who was adopted, and he looked so different from Ginger. I was just a kid, so I thought all kids looked like their parents, at least a little bit. They did on all the TV shows I watched. Ginger's dad introduced himself and told me, "Cassie, love makes a family. It's the only thing that matters."

I know my mom loves me. I know my dad

loves me. I always thought Ginger's dad was right, but something about my mom and dad living in different parts of the country means we'll no longer be a family. Right?

I spot Ginger and Nevin entering the courtyard and wave wildly. They both come over, but I can immediately tell it's not good.

"Where have you been? I called your cell and knocked on your door this morning until my knuckles hurt," Ginger says. Her tone is distinctly annoyed.

"You missed class today, and we have our big final at the science museum this week. We have to work together, Cassie," Nevin complains.

I pull the string on the box and open the lid to reveal the treats. "Look what I have!"

"Cannoli?" Ginger asks. I expect her tone to change dramatically, but it doesn't. She sounds just as annoyed as she did a few seconds ago.

"Yeah, cannoli. I figured it would help me tell you the bad news." I move my hands around the box like they do on old game shows.

Their expressions of anger melt into expressions of concern.

"What's wrong?" Ginger asks. Nevin is silent but keeps his eyes focused on me.

"Well, you know how we were going to go to the Jersey shore next week?"

"Yeah," they both say with a great deal of hesitation.

"But what do you mean *were* going to go?" Ginger asks.

"Well, I can't go." I frown to show my disappointment. The truth is, if there wasn't a chance I would be going to the Hamptons to see Rory next week, I would totally go with them. It's not my fault these two things are happening during the same week and on opposite beaches.

"Are you feeling okay?" Nevin asks.

"Oh, I'm fine," I say. "It's just that, well, Rory asked me to go to the Hamptons and, well, he and I are really getting along. And Ginger, we've gone to the beach loads of times."

"But we made plans," she says. "What about the Starfish Grill? And Ming-wei is going to be at the shore and . . ."

"I know," I say. But I don't know what to say after that. I knew I wouldn't have a lot to say, which is why I brought the treats. "Here." I grab a cannoli out of the box. "Have a cannoli."

"I don't want a cannoli!" Ginger snaps.

"Geesh, what's wrong with you?" I ask, knowing full well the answer to my question.

"It's what's wrong with *you*. Look, Cassie, I know you have a lot going on, but you can't just cover it all up with smiles and not talking about it and—and—" Ginger is almost in tears, and the sight of this makes me feel awful. She finally croaks out the last word, "Cannoli!" and then storms out of the courtyard, leaving Nevin and me alone.

There is a long silence, and then in one rapid movement he takes off his backpack and opens it. "We got our quizzes back. Here's yours." He hands me a familiar-looking piece of paper with a giant red *C* on it.

"Great," I say, taking it from him. "Could this day get worse?"

"Well," Nevin says, "Mr. Evans did say that you could still get a decent grade in class if you do well on the final. And you do have the smartest lab partner in class, and I know that science center inside and out."

"Yeah, about going to the science center," I say,

drawing out each word to delay the inevitable.

"What about it?" he asks.

"Let's just say the beach isn't the only place I won't be going." I tell Nevin that I won't be at the science center tomorrow. I explain that I booked this very major campaign. I almost tell him that this is my last chance to be part of a happy family. Even if it is totally pretend and just for a day. I think Nevin might be the one person in the world who would understand, but still I keep these thoughts to myself.

After I am done explaining, Nevin shakes his head and says, "But milady, me doth think that the science center is the pinnacle for scientific investigation." I sigh. It was so nice to have Nevin talking like a regular person for a while. Now he is back to full-blown Nerdlish. "Underestimated it c-c-cannot be, my fair maiden." Nevin stumbles a bit through the words, and then I realize he really only speaks this way when he's nervous. It's like he has to do this to get through a difficult situation. All summer, whenever he was just hanging out with me, or on a break from school without a lot of other kids around, he talked normally for the most part. Now I finally get it. Not only does

Nevin understand me, but I also think I understand him.

"Nevin, look. You've really helped me this summer, maybe more than you know, but I—just—I mean—I can't. This is just something I have to do." I don't want to hurt Nevin or Ginger, but I already made my decision. I know if I stay talking to Nevin even a second longer I might change my mind, so I run out of the courtyard, leaving Nevin alone and confused.

CHAPTER 45

The day of the Happy Family shoot I wake up feeling guilty. Usually guilt is something that grows over the day, but this morning it wakes me up like a hungry puppy. I know I should have turned down this booking, but I just couldn't. The call time on the cruise ship is a few hours earlier than the start time for the final project at the science center, so that means I need to lie to my mother about where I'm going.

During breakfast I barely utter a word, and when I grab my bag to head out, she says, "Good luck on your final!" I almost break down in tears. But once I shut the door of our apartment behind me, I realize there is no turning back. At this point what can I do? I've already told Honey I would be there.

I take the bus that stops a few blocks away from our apartment all the way up the West Side to the pier on the water. I have to cross under the highway to get to the location, and when I emerge on the other side, the sight takes my breath away. The location today is not some brightly lit set at a television studio in Queens. Today we are shooting on the *Neptune*, the largest, newest, and most beautiful ship in the Happy Family Cruise Line. Even though it is a gray day with some light rain, the gleaming white ship outshines everything.

Well, almost everything.

Ginger and I have never fought before, not really. I don't know what to do. It gives me a pit in my stomach that I can't make go away. And Nevin. I never thought I could feel bad about Nevin, but I can't help thinking of him eating breakfast right now and getting ready to go to the science center this afternoon without his partner, while I am boarding one of the most beautiful cruise ships in the world.

The *Neptune* is a masterpiece. It's hard to believe something this massive can float. I walk up the staircase that leads to the entrance, and the ship seems to grow in front of me. When I walk through the passenger portal, I arrive at a ten-story atrium with water slides, shops, and cafés. A glass elevator with blue, purple, and green lights moves from floor to floor of the wonderland.

I'm simply in awe, staring at the fantasy of it all, when a woman in her twenties wearing a scarlet red raincoat comes over to me and says, "You must be Cassie."

"Are you the assistant director in charge of minors?" I ask.

"Right you are. I guess you've been through this before, but just in case, let me show you where to sign in and get you settled in one of the dressing rooms. All the production stuff like wardrobe, makeup, and craft services is on the Calypso deck, and all the dressing rooms are there too. Here's your schedule for the day."

She hands me a few sheets of paper with my name on the top of them. Immediately, everything I've been feeling for the past few days goes away. I have in my hands the schedule for the day, and I don't have to worry about what to do or what to say. I don't even have to worry about how to feel. I look down at the schedule and see my scenes call for a "happy, carefree tween daughter," and that is exactly who I plan to be.

I look over everything very carefully. I notice

that all my scenes will shoot in the morning and that I will be done by lunch. I flip through the papers and see that Rory and the other cruise passengers are scheduled to arrive later in the morning, and his scenes shoot in the afternoon. This is the best news I have had in a while. I'll be able to hang out with him and talk about meeting him in the Hamptons. Maybe I made the right choice after all.

Knowing that I'm going to see Rory later makes the morning fly by.

I head over to wardrobe and makeup, where I meet my new family for the day. Of course, Ashley is playing my mom today, and a very handsome guy a little older than Ashley with some patches of gray in his hair is playing my dad. A kid a few years younger than me is playing my brother, and as we are having our final fitting, he turns out to be a bit of a pest, but since I imagine most younger brothers are a bit obnoxious, I don't mind.

The first scene of the day takes place by the pool and shows the happy family enjoying some colorful drinks and eating nachos. My wardrobe for this scene is a floral print rash guard and some brightly colored board shorts. The director meets us in the makeup room to tell us what we're going to do, and

I realize it's still only 8:10 a.m. I wonder how easy it will be to enjoy a plate of nachos at this hour.

I come out of makeup, and the previously gray sky is absolutely black and pouring sheets of rain. Of course, this doesn't stop the shoot. The production team has rigged a huge tarp over one of the pools where we will be filming, so it remains perfectly dry. The lack of sun isn't an issue when you have megawatt lights that create artificial light as bright as a sunny day and more reliable.

When you are on set, even the weather is something you can control.

I spend the next hour part of a happy family. They get about a dozen shots of the mom, dad, son, and daughter lounging by the pool, eating some snacks. We even play shuffleboard. They shoot us in one of the cabins playing a board game and in the restaurant eating dinner. I thought this moment of commercial bliss would solve all my problems, but today the usual magic doesn't have the same sparkle. I'm not lost in the world of the commercial. I'm simply playing my part. By midmorning we get a break, and I go change into my wardrobe for my last scene of the day, on the dance floor of the ship's dining room.

I go to the rack where all my costumes are hung and look for the dress I'm supposed to wear. I don't see it, so I ask the wardrobe mistress, a tightly wound woman with a beehive hairdo named Doris.

"Have you seen my dress?" I ask her.

She comes over and searches the rack and then says, "Oh, I forgot. Channing has it in the wardrobe room. It's not on the rack. Would you mind running down and just changing down there? I'm up to my eyeballs in elastic seams."

"Sure," I say.

I walk down the center staircase of the ship and back to the Calypso deck, where I go directly to the rooms they are using for wardrobe. As I turn the corner I see Faith. I haven't seen her at any auditions for a while, and I don't think she was at the callback, but I guess she must have booked one of the spots.

"Oh, hey, Cassie. I really thought they would have booked Phoebe in this spot," she says. It's a typical Faith comment. Not exactly nice, but nothing too nasty that I can put my finger on.

"Hi, Faith," I say, and ignore her comment. "Are you headed to wardrobe too?"

"Yeah," she says, and then raises her arm to point. "It's just down this hallway—" she starts.

"I know where it is. I'll see you there," I say, and walk away.

Channing recognizes me from my size card, and when he sees me, he says, "Hi, Cassie. Did Doris send you down for the new dress?"

"Yes." I say, and he walks over to a wardrobe rack where all shapes and sizes of garments are hanging and waiting to be plucked out of the lineup and featured on camera. The rack is tightly packed, so it takes Channing a minute to find my dress among the eligible contestants.

"Here it is!" he says, turning around and draping a garment bag with the dress over his arms. "The director said he wants you to sparkle, so we picked this."

"Thank you," I say, taking the bag from him.

"I'm doing some last minute fits, Cassie. Would you mind just changing here to make sure everything is perfect?"

"No problem," I say, and make my way past the girls who are still being fitted and push back the curtain on the dressing room to get changed.

Once I'm in the dressing room, I hang the garment bag on the hook next to the full-length mirror and carefully unzip the bag. Before I even have the zipper halfway down, I can tell this dress is something special. I take the dress out of the bag and just stare at it on the hanger for a second. It's so beautiful it almost takes my breath away.

The strapless top is made of hand-sewn rhinestones and small silver beads that glitter and make the light dance. The waist has a pewter sash with a matching fabric rose, and the skirt is so round and full that it looks like rolling hills covered in fresh snow. I hold it up against my body and admire the ensemble briefly before putting it on.

Once I have the dress on, I examine myself in the mirror to make sure everything is perfect. I'm adjusting the flower on the sash when I hear Faith's voice on the other side of the curtain say, "Hey, Rory. You finally showed up. How you doing?"

Rory is here.

I get a lump in my throat. I can't wait to see him. I'm about to push back the curtain when I hear him say, "Hey, Monique, I'm doing great since you're here."

I freeze.

My heart sinks.

Is it possible that there is a girl on the other side of this curtain who is actually named Monique and she happens to have a voice that sounds *exactly* like Faith's? A bunch of the girls on the other side of the curtain giggle, but then one of the girls says, "Her name's not Monique. It's Faith."

Then I hear Rory say, "I know. It's just an inside joke."

I can't believe it. How many insides does this guy have? Apparently more than one.

He totally played me with that stupid Monique line, and I fell for it. Then I hear Monique—or rather Monique *number two*—say, "Oh, Rory, I asked my parents about going to the Hamptons next week and . . ."

What? He asked her to go to the Hamptons too? I can't believe it. I want to tear open the curtain and confront him, but I keep hearing him chatting it up with Faith, and instead of getting angry, I just get very hurt and sad.

One of the assistant directors comes into the room and says he needs all the background players on set. I hear the room clear out. Everyone leaves, except me. In one moment my picture-perfect world has crumbled.

Rory has totally played me. What a jerk. What an incredible jerk. I knew somewhere in the back of my mind that Rory was just too good to be true. Why did I let myself believe him? Was I so blinded by his charm and smiles that I couldn't figure out what was really going on? I guess I'll never learn that things are not always what they appear to be. I lean back against the wall of the dressing room and slowly slump to the floor as my tears fall on to the glittering rhinestones of my costume.

CHAPTER 46

"*Let's go back to opening places,*" *the director* yells after the take, and everything on the set sort of reverses to the spot it was in just a few minutes back. I wish I could just snap my fingers like the director and reverse everything to whatever point in time I wanted. How far back would I go? To this morning? To last week? To the start of the summer? To before my parents started fighting? Unfortunately, I don't have this superpower.

Somehow I was able to drag myself off the floor of the dressing room, stop by makeup for a retouch, and make it to set all without having to talk to Rory or even look at Faith. Of course Rory tried to come over to me and say hello, but I ran in the opposite direction. I never want to see him again. At least now we're in the middle of shooting, so he won't be able to say anything to me that isn't in the script.

Usually I love repeating something over and over on set, but today has been too much. We are shooting my final scene of the day on the dance floor of the dining room. All I want to do is say my lines, hit my mark, change out of this wardrobe, wash off this makeup, and go home. But when the cameras roll I can barely get the words out.

Everything is so confusing, and everything seems so fake. This isn't my family. They're just actors who barely know me. This mom didn't sleep overnight with me at the hospital when I was six and had my tonsils out, and this dad didn't teach me how to skateboard without falling over.

I'm supposed to see my "mom" from across the dance floor, run over to her, give her a hug and say, "This is the best vacation ever. Let's never go home." On the last take I said, "This is the ever home vacation. Let's never go best." The director yelled, "Cut!" and everyone freaked out for a bit, because it seemed like I was speaking in tongues.

Every time I run toward Ashley I think about how happy I was this morning to have her playing my fake mom, and now all I want to do is see my mom, my *real* mom. Her haircut may not be as stylish as Ashley's, and she may not look like some director's fantasy of what a mom should look like, but she is *my* mom.

This morning in makeup I told Ashley how I bought my mom the same locket she was wearing at that audition a few months ago. Ashley told me that she would have given me the locket she had, but she threw it out. Apparently all the "young moms" are wearing pearls right now, not lockets, so Ashley just put hers in the trash, because she wouldn't be "caught dead" wearing something like that on the street. I didn't think too much about it when she told me this, but now it makes me sad. I thought the locket was pretty, and I know my mom would never throw it out. To my mom it's something special; to Ashley it's just a prop.

We do six more takes of the same exact line until I get it right. When I finally do I think everyone is so relieved they'll start doing a little cheer. I look at my watch. Even if I run full speed over to the subway, I'll never make it to the science center in time. I can't believe I've been acting like such an idiot. If only my mom was here right now, I'd tell her exactly how sorry I am.

I change back into my street clothes, take off my makeup, walk onto the deck of the ship, and just stare out across the water to the skyline. The clouds are finally beginning to lift, but it's too late, since I just spent the last few hours in manufactured sunshine.

I look down the other side of the ship toward the pier, and there in the parking lot, I suddenly recognize something. It's our little lemon-yellow VW bug and my mom standing next to it. "Mom! Mom!" I yell. She sees me and yells back.

I run across the deck and right into the assistant director. I beg her to tell me that I'm cleared for the day, and when she tells me I am, I continue running and don't stop until I am all the way off the boat and hugging my mom. "Mom, I'm so sorry. For everything." Tears start pouring out of my eyes. "I've been acting like a jerk. I'm sorry."

My mom takes me in her arms and hugs me. It's a real hug too, not like the ones you do on camera, where you have to hold your head up so your microphone doesn't get smothered or your makeup smeared. I let my tears fall on my mother's shirt as she gently pats her hand on my back.

"Cassie," she says. "You're my daughter and I love you as much today as I did the day in the hospital when you were born. I know everything that's going on is hard, but we'll get through it. All of us. You. Me. Your dad. We will *all* get through it. I promise."

I wipe some of the tears from my eyes and say, "Can we go home, Mom? Can we just go home?"

"Home? Not yet. If we jump in the car at this very second and head over to the science center, you can still participate in your final."

The science final! I leap toward the car and practically pull the handle off the door. I open the door, and there in the backseat is Ginger! I let out a squeal of both surprise and delight. "I hope you're not mad at me," she says quietly.

"Mad at you? Are you insane? You should be furious at me," I tell her. "I acted like a total jerk the other day in the courtyard. Actually, all summer. You've been trying to talk to me about my parents and everything and I just shut you out. I'm so sorry. It was just easier not to think about it."

"I know," Ginger says, nodding.

"But I'm done avoiding reality."

For a second I think back to an hour or so ago when I was slumped behind the dressing room curtain after hearing Rory call Faith "Monique." If that is supposed to be my picture-perfect world, I'll take my best friend and reality any day. I hug

Ginger like I haven't seen her in a year.

"Well," Ginger says, "I'm just glad you aren't mad at me. I figured you were at the cruise booking and when your mom asked me where you were, I told her you were here. I just thought you might be able to make it to meet Nevin." Nevin! He's someone I owe an apology to big-time.

"Ginger, that's why you're my best friend. Because sometimes you know what I need even when I don't." I grab onto the handle that my mom has fastened to the door with masking tape and glue, and it falls off in my hand. My mom drives out of the parking lot and speeds across town to the science center, while the three of us laugh hard at the fact that I am holding the severed car door handle in my hand. My life is anything but picture perfect, but maybe, just maybe, that's okay.

CHAPTER 47

I never want summer to end until the last few days of August. Something always happens just a day or so before school begins to get me excited for the new year. Usually I wake up one morning and there is just a hint of autumn coolness in the air, or I'm walking down the street and pass a particularly compelling back-to-school sale. This year I'm even more ready for school to start. I know I spent part of my vacation in class, but I'm definitely ready for a new beginning.

The night before the first day of school I'm sitting at the kitchen table with my mom, putting the finishing touches on my presents for Ginger and Nevin. She's taken out almost every single crafting supply she owns and is helping me embellish the two frames I bought for my friends. At first I was just going to frame the picture from our time at the beach and wrap it up, but I realized it needed something. It needed to be more than just a picture frame, and my mom suggested she help me transform it. Usually I'm against anything that involves a hot glue gun, but when I looked at the photo from the beach in the simple white frame, it looked too generic and boring. We had an amazing week at the shore, and I want my present to remind them of how special it was.

"See," my mom says, picking up a pale purple shell from the pile I have laid out next to the frame. "If you just sand the back of the shell with an emery board, it will stick better to the frame." I take the shell from her, sand the back of it gently, and apply a few small dots of glue before pressing it against the white frame. Quickly the store-bought frame becomes something very personal.

"I think these yellow shells would look good here," I tell my mom. She nods her head in agreement and hands me some bright pink sequins that she thinks Ginger would like and a little plastic surfboard that she suggests I use for Nevin's. With each dot of hot glue, I think about what good friends both Ginger and Nevin have been to me.

If it wasn't for Ginger telling my mom about

my predicament on that horrible day, I would never have made it from the shoot all the way across town to the science center. My mom basically drove like she was competing in the Indy 500. Behind the wheel she usually acts like she's teaching a driver's ed class, but that day she flew down the city streets so fast Ginger and I had to hold on to our seats and each other. I still remember the sound of the car brakes screeching as we came to a grinding halt at the entrance. I ran through the doors and up the stairs just in time to find Mr. Evans handing out our assignments for the final.

Nevin was walking over to Mr. Evans when I tapped him on the shoulder and said, "Well, I certainly hope you weren't planning on conducting these experiments by yourself. Your calculations might be flawless, but your lab report will need some style." Nevin was so shocked that he couldn't say anything. He looked like he'd just swallowed one of his calculators. We got to working right away, but when we took a break for lunch I apologized and explained everything. I thought he would be mad, but he actually understood. He was just thrilled I would be going to the beach with everyone.

I pick up a shell with a bumpy and rough surface to glue on the frame, but when I turn it over I see that it has a beautiful glossy blue-and-white-striped side. I realize it's perfect for Nevin's frame. Up until this summer I thought he was one-sided. I thought he was just this geeky kid who has always been part of my life, but now I know there's another side to him. He's actually my friend.

I see that my mom has a packet of red and pink paper hearts next to her. "Could I use those?" I ask.

"Sure," she says, handing the hearts and the bottle of regular glue to me. "This glue should work fine with those."

"Thanks, Mom." I take out a few of the hearts and alternate the red and pink ones on one side of the frame. For a second I think about writing Ginger and Ming-wei in the hearts, but my handwriting isn't neat enough. I'm so glad Ginger and Ming-wei are finally going out. When we all went out together down at the shore, it was obvious that Ming-wei is really into her. Ginger just needed a little boost of confidence, so I was glad I could be with her on her first group date.

The phone rings, and my mom picks it up. I hear her say a cordial hello, and then she says, "Well, of course, Michael. That's very nice of you. Hold on." She puts the phone to her chest to cover the speaker and says, "It's your dad. He wants to wish you luck on your first day of school."

I'm still not happy that my parents are getting divorced, but at least I'm dealing with the reality. I know thousands of kids survive this sort of thing, and the only way to really cope is to be honest about the situation and have friends who support you. Since I've been handling it better, my parents have actually been nicer to each other. I know there is little chance of them getting back together, but if the divorce means we can all be in the same room for five minutes without any fighting, maybe it's okay.

"Hi, Dad," I say into the phone.

"Hey, Peanut. Tomorrow's a big day. I just wanted to wish you luck."

"Thanks, Dad. But can I call you back? I'm supposed to meet Ginger and Nevin in the courtyard and I can't be late." I promise to call him back later and hang up the phone. My mom makes sure the frames are dry and helps me put them in a box.

I head out the door and walk quickly to the

courtyard, where I see Ginger and Nevin sitting on the same bench where I messed everything up a few weeks ago.

"Hey, guys," I say, holding out the box.

"What's in the box?" Nevin asks.

"Wow!" Ginger says, giggling. "There must be, like, a hundred cannoli in there."

All three of us laugh, since the box could probably hold more than that. "It's nothing you can eat," I tell them. "Well, at least nothing you could eat without having to make a trip to the emergency room. Here," I say, and put the box on the seat next to the bench. I take out each of their frames and hand them to my friends.

They both immediately start talking about how much they like the presents.

"I love this frame. It's so cute," Ginger says.

"Wow. This is very cool," Nevin echoes.

"I just wanted to do something to say thanks and, you know, make something to help us remember what a good time we had."

"This photo is quite remarkable," Nevin says, and holds the frame a little closer to his face. "When did we take it?" he asks.

"Don't you remember? It was the afternoon my

parents came down with Cassie's mom," Ginger tells him.

"That's right," I say. One afternoon they all came down from the city. Ginger's dad put his camera on a tripod and took a picture of the entire group. We are all on the deck of the house, and you can see the ocean and the sand in the background.

"I love it, Cassie. I really do," Ginger says. Nevin nods, and I smile.

"I made a frame for myself, too, and I already have it hanging next to my bed." They thank me for the presents, and we spend the rest of the evening talking about what teachers we hope we'll get and wishing that we'll all have the same lunch period.

That night, before I go to sleep, I look at the frame next to my bed. The picture makes me smile, but it's quite an unusual collection of individuals. There is Nevin's dad, who is wearing a bright blue Hawaiian shirt with hibiscus flowers, standing next to Nevin's stepmom, Mercedes. His stepbrother's dark skin stands out against his white T-shirt with the flag of the Dominican Republic on it. Ginger's dad is almost completely covered, since his fair skin burns easily, and her mom's wheelchair has an umbrella attached to it to provide even more shade for them. My mom is next to them, wearing a blue sundress and the locket I gave her with my picture in it. Ginger, Nevin, and I have just come out of the pool, so we are dripping wet, but our faces are beaming smiles at the camera lens.

Even if you really studied the picture, you might not be able to tell who is related to whom and how we all know one another, but in a second you could tell that we are a family and that there is love. The image is a bit blurry and off center, but I cherish it. It may not be picture perfect, but it is a perfect picture.

The drama continues—on camera and off!—in

COMMERCIAL BREAKS,

Dramatic Pause

"Nicole didn't do it. I did it!" I yell. I can feel the space vibrating from the intensity in my voice. I swallow hard, then take out the red-stained knife from the left pocket of my blue gingham dress and hold it up to everyone. I can hear a few people gasp. I watch the light bounce off the shiny plastic tip before throwing it on the table.

"I killed Harriet Conners because she knew the secret," I say calmly, as if I'm explaining that there might be a slight chance of rain tomorrow. Then it hits me. My eyes widen and I stare at the knife on the table as if it's a cobra about to strike. I look at all of the people around me and scream, "I killed Harriet Conners because she knew what happened. She knew what happened on the seesaw!"

I fall to my knees. First I am just quietly weeping, then I am sobbing, and then I become fully hysterical and collapse flat on the floor. I can hear gasps of horror all around me now that everyone knows the truth. Tears pour out of my eyes, and my body writhes on the floor like piece of bacon in a steely hot frying pan. I pound my fists and kick my feet for a few seconds before coming back up to my knees and screaming at the top of my lungs, "I did it! I KILLED HARRIET CONNERS! "

For a few small seconds there is complete silence. An undeniable tension saturates everyone and everything.

Then I hear a familiar creaking from above me. Without even looking up I know the heavy red velvet curtain is beginning to fall. I don't stop crying until the golden fringe has hit the floor of the stage, and even then I give it one last good sob. Then I hear the most beautiful sound in the world. Applause. The thick curtain muffles the thunder, but I can still tell the audience is going wild. The lights flip from the warm, carefully constructed pools of illumination intended to highlight the drama onstage to the workday fluorescent lights that help the actors move around backstage. Intermission is only fifteen minutes long, and the entire set needs to change from classroom to courtroom.

I quickly get out of the way so the stage crew can get to work.

I wipe the stage tears from my eyes, and as soon as I do, I notice real tears are at the ready just behind them. I can't believe this is my final performance in this very special show.

I've been playing the role of Kimberly Ann Fortunato, the girl who lies, cheats, and schemes to cover up the murder of her former best friend turned middle-school rival, Harriet Conners, in the off-Broadway production of *Seesaw for One* for the past four months. We were originally scheduled to run for only one month but my performance won rave reviews in all the press, with one theater critic going so far as to say, "Isabel Marak Flores delivers a powerful and truthful performance that is NOT to be missed."

Of course, theater is a group effort. Everyone from the wardrobe mistress to the director has a part in creating the onstage magic, so no one artist can ever take credit for the success of a production. It's a team sport, and sometimes that's the part I like best—a whole group of artists pulling together to create something beautiful and meaningful for an audience. Still, it was wonderful to be noticed for my work. I was especially satisfied that the critic called my work "truthful." For an actor, that is the ultimate compliment. Acting isn't just pretending and playing dress-up. It's an art form just like painting or sculpture. It takes discipline, dedication, and seriousness to do it well.

I have only a short bit of time between the curtain going down on act one and the curtain going up on act two, and I not only have to change, but I also have to do my vocal exercises and my meditation. While act one ends with my dramatic confession, act two is really where I put my dramatic skills to the test, so I need to be prepared. In the upcoming courtroom scene, I deliver a seven-minute monologue about what led me to kill Harriet. If I'm very quiet after my final line I can usually hear a few people in the audience crying. Once I heard a woman sobbing so loudly I was worried I wouldn't be heard over her. The writer of *Seesaw for One* has done a brilliant job, and I am so honored that my performance has the ability to move the audience to tears. Isn't that what any artist wants—to move people?

"Isabel, that was amazing. Your best performance yet," Alan Jackson says to me as I make my way backstage towards my dressing room on the upstairs balcony. Mr. Jackson is the director and selected me to play the role of Kimberly. He is the recipient of two Tony nominations and debuted his one-man show at Lincoln Center to standing ovations a few years ago. I respect him very much and I'm very grateful he believes in me.

"Thank you, Mr. Jackson," I tell him. "I've learned so much from you as a director." He walks next to me, and on the way to the dressing room we pass the curtains that kept the actors hidden from the audience.

"Well, I hope you will continue to learn," he says.

"What do you mean?" I ask.

Before he can answer, Hilda, the woman who coordinates the costumes, hair, and makeup for everyone interrupts us. "Sorry, Mr. Jackson, I just need to put her hair in a bun for the opening of act two in the courtroom."

"Oh, of course," Mr. Jackson says. "Isabel, I probably shouldn't tell you anything until after tonight's performance anyway. Closing night nerves, I guess. Go ahead, Hilda." There is not enough time during intermission to sit in a proper hair and makeup chair and be done up. Hilda just grabs an actor where she can and does what she needs to do. Backstage is always chaos, but it is an organized chaos that I love.

Hilda steps behind me and starts brushing my hair, but I can't help wondering what Mr. Jackson meant.

"Is everything okay, Mr. Jackson?" I ask. "Did I do something wrong?"

"Oh heavens, no. Everything is fine," he says, and strokes his gray beard with his hand. During rehearsals I noticed he strokes his beard like this when he is in deep thought about something important. An actor has to be aware of every behavior she encounters in case she wants to use it for a character at some point in the future. I realize it's unlikely that I'll play a character with a gray beard in the near future, but still it is important to be observant.

"You haven't done anything *wrong* at all. In fact, you've been doing everything right. Quite right indeed."

Hilda takes one last sweep with her hand, pulls my hair into one long piece, and then wraps it around into a tight bun that she fastens with a few bobby pins before lightly spraying the back of my head with some hairspray. Mr. Jackson quietly watches the transformation.

"You're all set, Isabel. Knock 'em dead." She pauses and adds, "Oh, wait. You already did that." She laughs at her own joke and Mr. Jackson and I join in. Everyone is in a playful mood on closing night.

"Thanks, Hilda," I say, and she rushes off to get another actor changed or coifed for act two. "Great work," Mr. Jackson adds.

Mr. Jackson and I quickly climb the stairs to my dressing room. Once we are at the top, I look down at the stage and see that the army of a stage crew is in the middle of its orchestrated set change. A few men attach ropes to the walls of the classroom, and with a quick signal the walls suddenly float straight up past the balcony area where the dressing rooms are to the rafters of the theater, as the walls of the courtroom slowly descend from their perch above the stage. The crew on the ground holds their arms out, waiting for the arrival of the new scenery, prepared to safely secure it into place. I know actors work with precise timing, but sometimes I think we should keep the curtain up during intermission so the audience could see just how much work goes into the set change. In my opinion, it is just as precise and challenging as everything else that happens onstage, and as my father says, "Where there is beauty, there is art."

I walk into my dressing room and, Sean, the stage manager, who I think was born with a walkie-talkie headset attached to him, walks by, knocks on the doorframe, and without missing a step says, "We are at ten minutes until the opening of act two, Miss Isabel."

"Ten minutes, thank you," I say. It's protocol in the theater to acknowledge any time cue from the stage manager.

"Isabel, I should let you prepare," says Mr. Jackson from the doorway, "but I just want you to know that there are some very important people in the audience tonight. *Very* important." He scrunches his eyebrows together when he says the second *very important*, and I think maybe this eyebrow scrunching is a behavior I should also make note of.

"Thank you for letting me know" I say. Since we've gotten such good press, we have had a steady stream of celebrities at the show, from Hollywood A-listers to politicians. Last week we had the winner of some superpopular reality-TV game show in the audience, and Ruth Punjabi, who plays Harriet

Conners's mother, was so excited she could barely remember her lines. When she asked me if it made me nervous, I just told her no. The truth is my family doesn't even own a TV, so I had absolutely no idea who this guy was. Even if I did know, it doesn't matter who is sitting out there in the dark. An audience is an audience, and my job is simply to give the best performance I can no matter who is out there.

I remind Mr. Jackson about this since I don't want him to think he has thrown off my performance. "It doesn't matter to me, Mr. Jackson. I'm totally focused tonight."

"That's what I was expecting you to say. I know you have to get ready for act two and I should not have disturbed your, preparation. I know you take it very seriously."

"I do," I say.

"Just meet me at the stage door after the performance tonight when you're out of wardrobe and makeup. All I'll say is that there is someone I would like you to meet."

"Okay. I'll be there," I say, and he tells me to break a leg in act two and heads back down the steps. I close the door to my dressing room so that I can do my preparations. I look at the clock over the bouquet of perfect daisies my parents sent me and see that I have just enough time.

I know I have to stay focused, but sometimes the serious actor inside me collides with the thirteen-year-old girl inside me. I wonder who Mr. Jackson wants me to meet that is so important that he decided to come backstage during intermission to tell me. Is it a celebrity? A personal friend? A theater critic? I shuffle through the possibilities in my mind for about eight seconds.

"We are at five until the opening of act two, Miss Isabel," Sean says as he raps his knuckles on my dressing room door.

"Five minutes, thank you," I say loud enough so he can here me on the other side of the door.

I shake the possibilities of who Mr. Jackson wants me to meet out of my head. It's time for my two-minute meditation exercise and short vocal warm-up before act two. It doesn't matter who he wants me to meet, because from now until the final curtain falls, I'm not Isabel Marak Flores. I'm Kimberly Ann Fortunato, and I'm about to go on trial for murder. . . .

ABOUT THE AUTHOR

P. G. Kain has been on hundreds and hundreds of commercial auditions for everything from a talking taco to a mad cupcake scientist. He has even booked a few spots. He is on faculty at New York University, where he is the chair of Contemporary Culture and Creative Production in Global Liberal Studies. As a Faculty Fellow in Residence at NYU, P. G. lives among nine hundred undergraduate students in a residence hall near Gramercy Park. You can reach P. G. and get commercial tips at www.TweenInk.com.

Did you **LOVE** this book?

Want to get access to great books for **FREE?**

Join

Simon & Schuster

IN THE

bookloop

<u>where you can</u>

✷ Read great books for FREE! ✷

⣰ Get exclusive excerpts ⣰

§ Chat with your friends ⧨

◉ Vote on polls ◉

Log on to 🔗 everloop.com
and join the book loop group!

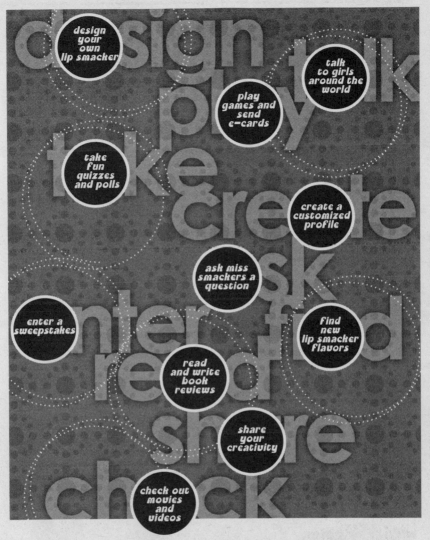

IF YOU ♥ THIS BOOK,

you'll love all the rest from

YOUR HOME AWAY FROM HOME:

AladdinMix.com

HERE YOU'LL GET:

- ♥ The first look at new releases

- ♥ Chapter excerpts from all the Aladdin M!X books

- ♥ Videos of your fave authors being interviewed

Aladdin ♥ Simon & Schuster Children's Publishing ♥ KIDS.SimonandSchuster.com